WRIGHT KIND OF TROUBLE

WRIGHT KIND OF TROUBLE

WRIGHT DUET BOOK ONE

K.A. LINDE

PART I

WEDDING

1

HARLEY

MARCH

"You look like you're going to a funeral."

I blinked at my brother and then gestured to my black lace dress. "Excuse me?"

Whitton shook his head as he squared off his perfectly knotted silk tie. "I know you wanted to be Winona Ryder, growing up, but don't you think this is taking it a little too far? You look like that girl from *Beetlejuice*."

"Should I be insulted or flattered that you think I look like Lydia?" I asked with a tilt of my head.

He laughed. "Only you, Harley."

"Black is fine for a wedding. It's a neutral color. You're going in a black suit!"

"I could wear charcoal," he said with a shrug.

I turned back to the living room mirror to check out the waves I'd put into my long blonde hair. "Don't be pedantic."

"Oh no, Harley is using her advanced vocabulary. You

must have upset her," Whitton's twin, Weston, said as he strode out of the kitchen with a coffee in hand.

My brothers couldn't be more opposites. If they didn't look exactly alike, no one would guess they were related. West was a laid-back musician with a go-with-the-flow vibe, and Whitt was all five-year plans, business suits, and strict schedules. The one thing they always agreed on was ganging up on me. But I could give as good as I could take.

"You're not even wearing a suit coat," I said then pointed at his feet. "And you're in Chucks."

Whitt winced as he looked at West's attire. "She has a point."

West raised his coffee to us. "Still wearing them."

"We could put you in a suit."

I grinned, having sufficiently distracted Whitt. And he was wrong anyway. I looked nothing like Lydia, as much as it dismayed me. I'd even forgone my normal Doc Martens for a pair of black heels that made my already-long legs look miles long. I'd contemplated a pair of white sneakers, but no way would Whitt have let me out of the house. Boy didn't understand fashion.

I slung my black bag over my shoulder and dug out my phone. I shot off a text to Mom.

Wedding bound. Make the boys stop arguing.

A second later, in lieu of a return text, Mom's face appeared on my screen. I clicked open on the video call.

"Hey, Mom."

Both of my brothers stopped talking and looked over at me. Well, mission accomplished.

"Hey, sweetie. Are you excited for Jordan's wedding?"

I shrugged. "Sure."

My mom shot me a quintessential mom look, her short blonde hair falling into her round face—which was my mirror, plus twenty-five years. "So eloquent, my little scholar."

"You should have come in for it."

It was her turn to be dismissive. "I don't know what your brother would have thought about that."

Which was fair.

Our family was...complicated.

To say the least.

See, our dad was a cheating bastard. In fact, he'd had a whole other family in Vancouver for years before he ever found our mom on a business trip in Seattle for Wright Construction, our family's namesake. Jordan and his younger brother, Julian, were his kids from his "real" family, and Whitt, West, and I were his dirty little secret. We'd all discovered it a few years ago and confronted Dad about it. I never wanted to talk to his lying face ever again. The boys were more conflicted. Though I didn't see what was conflicting about it. I'd never let someone treat me the way Owen Wright had treated my mom.

As luck would have it, Jordan and Julian had moved out of Vancouver to dry, dusty Lubbock, Texas, where the headquarters for the family business were located. West followed while pursuing his music. Then, I got a full-ride scholarship to Texas Tech University, and with the prospect of me leaving, Whitt had agreed to come too.

I'd felt bad leaving Mom behind in Seattle. We'd even tried to convince her to come with, but her job and friends and aging parents still lived in town. She'd spent her whole life there. Even if she wanted to move for us, she couldn't. Not yet at least.

"Hey, Mom!" West said, veering into the picture and waving.

Her eyes lit up. "West. I heard that you and your brother were bickering."

Whitt leaned over. "We were doing no such thing."

"Correct," West agreed. "Whitt was trying to dictate what I should wear."

Our mom's eyes raked his tie-less button-up. "Are you wearing Converse?"

Whitt and I both cracked up and said, "Yes," at the same time.

West shot us a dirty look.

"It's fine, Mom," he grumbled.

"I want you to dress appropriate for your brother's wedding," she said.

"You should have come," I told her. "Bonus mom!"

She laughed at that addition. "I'll come back down eventually. Just couldn't get away from work and Grandma."

I exchanged a look with my brothers. Grandma and Grandpa's health had been in decline for years. It was running Mom ragged. We all worried and missed her. The only time she'd come to visit was to move me into my dorm.

"Next time," Whitt said tactfully. "We should get going."

"Okay. Love you three. Have fun and send me pictures when you can!"

We all agreed that we would.

I hung up the phone and put it back in my purse. "Shall we?"

The boys nodded, and then we headed out to my little Kia. Mom had wanted to get me something fancier for the fucking horrid twenty-seven-hour drive from Seattle to Lubbock. But I knew that fancier meant money from Owen, which meant strings attached, which meant hell. So, I'd been happy with what we could afford. She'd served me well enough so far.

Not that Whitt agreed. "I should just drive the Lexus," he said, looking mournfully toward the garage where his shiny silver car rested.

"Sure," I said automatically. A wicked smile coming to my face. "And since I'm the DD, I can drive you all home in it later."

Whitt blanched. "Fine. No. You're not driving my car."

Whitt didn't let *anyone* drive his big-boy car. So, it was my Kia after all.

West piled into the backseat, and Whitt took the passenger as I sank into the driver's side and connected my phone. David Bowie blared through the speakers.

Whitt jerked to life and reached for the stereo. "Christ, do you even have eardrums at that volume?"

I blinked at him lazily. "Earsplitting is the only volume to listen to David Bowie."

"She's right," West agreed, putting his fist through the middle of the seats. I bumped him, and we both laughed at the look on Whitt's face.

Jordan and Annie's wedding was on the south side of town at the vineyard that Jordan and Julian had opened with their friend Hollin Abbey. The place had come a long way since its conception with award-winning wine and a booming event business. Jordan had told me once while I was touring the place that it had started as a line dancing dance hall and it was where he and Annie had first gotten together.

It was hard to picture that as I drove up to the immaculate venue. The barn that he'd told me had been half falling down was strong and sturdy with fresh wood stain and a new roof. The vineyards were in their first couple of weeks of bud-breaking, blooming green everywhere in the spring weather. The lawn between the barn and the cellar was a rich green and covered in white chairs and florals. The happy couple couldn't have asked for better weather. Lubbock was notoriously unpredictable in the spring, alternating between eighties and fifties, breezy days and dust storms, sunshine and flooding.

The parking lot was already packed with what looked like half of the town to celebrate the occasion. I parked at the back of the lot next to a fancy Porsche sports car.

West whistled at the shiny red exterior when he stepped out. "Nice ride," he said.

Whitt sucked his teeth. "My Lexus is just as nice."

"Be for fucking real," I muttered as I admired the car.

"This is a Porsche 718 Cayman," West said, his voice dripping with lust. He'd always wanted something like this. "This thing goes zero to sixty in less than five seconds. It tops out at a hundred seventy-something miles per hour."

"Come along before you have an orgasm over the thing." I pushed him in the back, and he shot me a look.

I grinned at him, and the three of us headed toward the vineyard.

"My car is just as nice," Whitt muttered again.

I patted his shoulder. "Keep telling yourself that."

"I wonder who it belongs to," West said. "Need to see if the guy will let me drive it."

"Excuse me. It could be a woman."

West laughed. "Sure, but it's probably not."

I looked to Whitt for help, but he just shrugged and agreed with West.

"Y'all are the worst. One day, I'm going to stop all this gendered shit from you two."

West threw his arm around my shoulders. "And one day, we're going to stop you from using the word *y'all* as if you're from the South."

I pushed him away with an eye roll. I'd adopted *y'all* as soon as I moved to Lubbock. It was superior to other options. My brothers were just ribbing me.

We stepped into line with the rest of the crowd. I'd only been in Lubbock for a few months and didn't know all of the Lubbockites. I'd met my Wright cousins—Jensen, Austin, Landon, Morgan, and Sutton—as well as their respective partners. The other guys at the vineyard were familiar, as well as the girls who were on the soccer team I'd subbed in exactly one game for. I'd played casually in high school, but my joy from the game had been more...social than fitness-related. Everyone else at the wedding was a relative stranger.

Including West's roommate, Nora, who he was super into. Even if he hadn't exactly admitted it.

Finally, we reached the front of the line. West and Whitt were engaging with the ushers while my eyes roamed the outdoor space. Now that I had a full view, I could tell they'd sunk *money* into this wedding. Good for them.

I turned to try to wrangle my brothers when my eyes landed on a guy dressed in a tailored navy suit. My breath caught at the sight of him. Beautiful and pouty and tortured perfection. The consternation that played across his bold features was at odds with the occasion. As if he'd walked into the wedding off the street and was trying to figure out what he was doing here.

The light played across the soft curl of his ash-blonde hair, highlighting the golden strands threaded through the darker color. His eyes were a blue that shouldn't be legal. Like falling into a pool of water. They kept glancing up at the altar and quickly away, as if he didn't want anyone to see him looking. His hand kept going to the inside pocket of his suit, like he needed whatever was in there for courage.

For a split second, it was as if he could feel my eyes upon him. His gaze swept in my direction, and then they locked upon me. My mouth went dry. My body felt like it had been electrified. Every nerve stood on end. Just from a glance.

With those high cheekbones, a razor-sharp jawline, and pretty, pouty lips opened slightly on a question, I was a goner.

I didn't even know his name.

"Harley," West called.

I jumped, breaking eye contact and turning back to my brother. "Huh?"

"Let's get our seats."

I nodded and followed them down the aisle, closer and closer to the man who had captured me in one look. I was still looking at him when I nearly ran into Whitt's back. He gave me a strange look and then turned into the row.

I was momentarily frozen as I saw that I was directly across from him. He caught my gaze again, and a smirk crossed his features. The first look that wasn't full of irritation. My stomach flipped, and heat came to my cheeks.

Then the music began. The wedding was about to start. His frown returned, bigger than ever, and he sank into his seat.

I quickly took mine, coming back to myself in increments.

I had no idea who he was.

He had to be ten years older than me.

My brothers would not be chill with this.

Fuck.

2

CHASE

The sun was shining, the birds were chirping, and I was at my ex's wedding as she married my enemy.

Annie stood at the front of the room with her hands in Jordan Wright's as a tear trickled down her cheek. Her friends and family were on all sides as she spoke her vows to the man she loved. The man who wasn't me.

My hand inched toward the flask in my coat pocket. It'd probably be rude to pull it out in the middle of the ceremony. Right?

I sighed and slouched back further.

It wasn't that I was still in love with Annie. We'd been best friends, growing up. We briefly dated in high school, and then, as I was off to Yale for my undergrad, we made a pact. If we weren't married by thirty, then...we'd marry each other. A part of me had always assumed that my person would be Annie. Now, I was twenty-nine and watching her marry someone else.

I was happy for her. In a way...because she was happy. Though not about *who* she was marrying. If it could have been *anyone* other than Jordan Wright, that would have been preferable. Considering the long-held rivalry between the Wrights and the Sinclairs, which had only doubled when they opened this winery and when Jordan fell for my girl, it was shocking that I'd even shown up.

I'd gotten some looks when I arrived.

But Annie had personally delivered the invite, and even if we weren't what we had been, we had too much history for me to deny her.

"You may now kiss your bride."

I bit back another sigh and forced myself to applaud as the crowd applauded their union.

Why couldn't I have just stayed home? It would have been easier. My own sister had told me I was a fool for going. She probably wasn't wrong.

Jordan grabbed Annie's hand in his and raised it high above his head. The crowd roared its approval, coming to their feet in a triumph of adoration. The crowning jewel of the Wrights, who were fucking royalty in this town. A fact that I very clearly remembered, as I was surrounded by them.

Still, I plastered a smile on my face as they hurried down the aisle. I'd never seen Annie so happy before. As if all of her dreams had come true.

I wanted that for her.

I wanted the joy on her face.

I wanted everyone cheering for her.

But I could be sad, even briefly, for what could have been. It wouldn't have worked out. I knew that now. But there had been a point in my life when I was sure it would be her. Instead, we were here.

She walked past me down the aisle without even a glance in my direction. Jordan Wright didn't even need to shoot me a smug look or anything. He'd won long ago. Not that it had been a competition. Her heart was her own. And it was easier to have this closure. She was married. Officially. Time to move on.

The rest of the party filed out after them. More Wrights. More of their dates. All happy as could be.

Then, it was my turn. I stepped into the aisle, and there she was.

I stopped abruptly in my tracks at the sight of the blonde who had been seated in the aisle across from me. I'd caught her looking at me when we first sat down, but I'd been too focused on what was happening in front of me to get more than a glance in her direction. And now... I couldn't stop looking.

Her black dress swished around her pale, toned thighs. A dress that was more in line with...a funeral than a wedding. A fact that felt oddly appropriate at the moment. But it fit her like a glove with tight boning around her narrow waist and a full skirt and billowy sleeves. Her hair was lighter than mine by only a few degrees, and it hung down past her shoulders in light waves. Her lips were pillowy with a little divot in the middle that made me want to sink my teeth into it. Her face was round and youthful with rosy cheeks, framed by the threads of her honey hair. Then, I landed on her eyes, and my entire world stalled out.

They weren't the blue of an ocean. But the ice of a glacier right before the boat collided and sank into the depths. Blue and gray and threads of silver that felt like they wrapped around my poor, bruised heart and forced it back to beating.

"Hi," I said before I could stop myself.

Her cheeks flushed a rosy pink that went straight to my balls. God, I wanted to make her blush again.

I wanted.

I just...wanted.

"Hey," she said with a quirk of her mouth.

We moved into step together, walking down the wedding aisle, almost touching shoulder to shoulder. The walk was only a few mere feet, and yet it felt like we were walking in slow motion. As if each step were a small eternity and I never wanted to wake up from whatever dream I'd just stumbled into.

"I like your dress."

Her smile widened. "Thanks. My brother said it looks like it's for a funeral."

"What's wrong with that?"

She liked that. I could see it in the way her eyes lit, and she listed sideways toward me. Our shoulders brushed, and electricity passed in the contact. A soft whoosh of air was sucked between those lush, succulent lips, and I felt my world leaning into that breath. As if she were uttering a siren call that wrapped me in her magic.

"So, you think it looks like a funeral dress?" she asked.

"You don't?"

"It's celebratory." She fluffed the skirt around her thighs. "See? Perfect for dancing."

"Maybe I'll find out later."

She grinned. "If you're lucky."

I was not.

Time had proven again and again that the Wrights had siphoned off all of my luck. Their Midas touch had only turned me to tin.

But for her, I'd pray to the god of luck.

"Chase," I offered, holding my hand out.

She slipped her dainty hand into mine. "Harley."

"Pleasure."

"All mine."

"Harley," a voice called behind us.

And then we were at the end of the aisle. Our universe expanded back to its original state. So much bigger than the microcosm we'd entered on our brief walk. I might as well have leprosy in this crowd. While our magnetism lingered in the air, something snapped.

"I'll catch you later," she said.

I wasn't sure if it was a promise or not, but I hoped to make her keep it.

She winked at me as she headed toward the person who had called for her. I didn't recognize them, but I hadn't been around this crowd much in the last year. They looked like Wrights. Tall, dark hair, broad shoulders. Jordan and Julian could easily pass as their brothers.

Was she dating a Wright? That would be just my luck.

I watched her walk away for another couple seconds before falling into the line of people headed into the Wright Vineyard barn. The room was decorated to the nines. Flowers and candles and some elaborate sheets overhead made the rustic barn look modern and festive.

Whoever had designed the thing had a knack for it. I'd gone to my fair share of New England weddings for Yale friends, and even they could hardly compare to the thought put into this. Of course, only the best for the Wrights.

Maybe one day, I wouldn't look at the whole town they ran with the spite of a conquered people.

I found a corner away from the rest of the crowd and let the open bar fill up. I took a slug of liquid courage from my flask and leaned back against the wood slats, pulling my phone out of my pocket.

I scrolled the texts from Ashleigh. There was more than a dozen, all getting increasingly more insane. She'd dated Julian Wright for two years, and after things had gone sour—thanks to her self-sabotage—she hated the Wrights even more than I did. Which was a feat.

I shot her a text back.

It was fine. Just waiting at the reception now.

A string of texts followed.

What is her dress like? Did you get a picture?

Is Julian there with anyone?

Does he look good?

I don't care. Never mind. Tell me about the vineyard. How is it done? Do you know who did the flowers?

I rolled my eyes and turned the vibrate off on my phone. I didn't need any more of *that* tonight. Today was hard enough without having to give her a play-by-play of it all while it happened. I had no doubt she'd show up at my house tomorrow and demand all the information she could get. Not sure why she bothered.

I sulked in the corner, watching the mingling. Normally, I was a social butterfly, but today was different. The temperature in the room had escalated, the longer we waited. Eyes glancing my way. Whispers passed in my direction. I felt like the pariah of a Jane Austen film.

A hush finally went over the crowd as the barn doors opened, revealing the bridal party.

My eyes skipped to the entrance as bridesmaids and groomsmen danced into the barn, and then I sighed, "Fuck it."

I walked away from the festivities and toward the now-empty bar line. I couldn't get drunk tonight. Not when I'd decided to drive here. It would have been smarter to call a cab or something, but I hadn't thought that I'd need more than the liquid courage of my flask. Turned out, I was wrong. I could use at least *one* drink to get through this dance, give Annie my well wishes— even if I didn't feel them—and then book it out of there. She probably didn't expect more than that from me anyway.

Just as I stepped up to the bar, Harley appeared in a flurry of black lace. My eyes slipped down her tall, lithe body. The figure of a dancer. My mind fell down a dirty hole, wondering if she was as flexible as a dancer. If she could move like one as easily as she had slipped into place in front of me for her drink. If that black lace dress hid black lace underneath.

I closed my eyes for a moment to try to eradicate that thought. She was a relative stranger and young.

That much I knew.

She was definitely young.

Yet she ordered a glass of red wine right in front of me, deliberating its merits with the bartender like a connoisseur. I'd guessed early twenties, but maybe mid-twenties with that attitude. I hadn't met many women who could discuss the merits of a fine wine at twenty-one. Only the old-money girls I'd met at Yale who'd suckled at the teat of wealth and overindulgence since childhood.

Harley didn't seem the type.

She turned around then. Her glass was half full of red wine, and she gasped as she nearly stumbled directly into me. The wine sloshed in the glass. On instinct, I reached out and slipped my hand around her wrist. It was narrow, the bones delicate under my grasp. It steadied her enough so that only one tiny drop fell onto the wooden flooring.

"I got you," I told her.

"My God," she muttered. "I didn't see you there."

I snatched a tiny white napkin with Annie's and Jordan's initials embossed in black and then bent a knee before her and swiped the red wine, like a smear of blood obscuring the letters. I glanced up at her from below, her eyes trained on me, and smirked. This was the view of a lifetime.

"No harm done."

"I suppose so. What are you drinking? I'll buy," she said with a wicked grin.

"It's an open bar."

"Exactly."

I laughed. A real one. Not the one that came with my forced smile. "All right. It's on you."

She eyed me curiously for a second before saying, "You seem like a Malbec person."

I startled. That was specific. "How'd you know?"

"You give off the vibe."

"What sort of vibe is that?"

"Mysterious," she said. "Dark fruit, smoky finish." She turned to the bartender and ordered a glass of wine for me.

I raised my eyebrows. "And you? What are you drinking?"

"Pinot noir, of course."

"Of course."

"Silky, enticing, but structured," she said, holding the glass aloft for me to look at.

But my eyes were all for her. The words coming out of her mouth sent me into that same tailspin spiral.

"I like a good pinot."

She laughed. "You like whiskey."

"I do," I agreed. "How do you know so much about wine?"

"My mom's Italian," she quipped, as if that explained everything. And maybe it did.

I took my Malbec from the bartender, dropping a twenty into the tip jar, and moved off to the side with Harley.

"So, how do you know the bride?" she asked after taking a sip of her wine.

I'd completely forgotten where we were.

I didn't know how she'd managed to make me forget. It was Annie's wedding day. I'd been dreading it for months. Yet here I was, at the start of something new. I found that I didn't want to tell Harley. I didn't want the pity to cross her face when she found out.

"Old friends," I said instead of the whole truth that had been on the tip of my tongue. "We went to high school together."

"Nice. Annie seems really sweet."

"And you?" I asked before we fell too far down that road. "How do you know the groom?"

She shrugged one shoulder. "He's my brother."

I wavered in place at that answer. Jordan Wright was...Harley's *brother*. Which made her...Harley Wright.

The little sister of my enemy.

I should walk away right now. Walk away and never look back. Because Jordan would *kill* me if he knew I was into his sister. And yet I couldn't find it in me to care.

A slow smile came to my face.

I shouldn't.

But oh, I was going to do it anyway.

3

HARLEY

"That right?" he said.

"Yeah, it's a long story."

I opened my mouth, prepared to give the long, sordid story of my father's duplicity, when a cheer went up in the crowd.

Chase and I turned toward the barn doors, where Annie and Jordan appeared in all their glory. Her dress was resplendent—a princess cut that made her look like she'd stepped out of a storybook. Her long red tresses framing her face. Jordan was enraptured. His eyes only for his bride.

We clapped at their entrance. When I peeked a glance in Chase's direction, I found his eyes on mine instead of the happy couple. My cheeks flushed again.

I wasn't ready to walk away from him.

From whatever was happening right now.

Yet I had no other choice. Dinner was being served.

He just smiled at me. "Save me a dance, remember?"

"I said if you were lucky."

His hand came to my wrist, and the contact sizzled. "Maybe luck is with me tonight."

My heart stuttered in my chest as he headed to his seat. I followed him as he made his way across the room. I didn't know what spell he'd cast over me, but it wove around me, knotting at the edges.

I found my seat, across the room from Chase, and listened with half an ear to my brothers and their dates. Nora and Eve sat on either side of West and Whitt and kept a happy rapport with the table. Dinner was slow and languid with a half-dozen toasts afterward. Everyone wanted to wish the couple the best.

Then came a series of wedding essentials. Nora plucked each off of a list and delivered them at the perfect moments—a first dance, cake cutting, bouquet toss.

Music shifted to something more up tempo, and I fell onto the dance floor with the rest of the girls. I'd purposely avoided it during the bouquet toss. No *way* was I going to be the next one married in *this* group. Screw that.

But the dancing was fun. It was my favorite part about going out on the weekends with my roommates. I'd hit a few frat parties first semester and promptly realized the only thing I liked about them was the dancing. The groping, drinking, and general aura of toxic masculinity were too much for me.

Still, I kept waiting for Chase to join us. But he'd disappeared at some point in the evening. I didn't know where exactly he'd gone off to, but I couldn't deny that I was disappointed.

The music slowed to a male pop ballad that had been all over the radio. Couples flooded the dance floor, and I slowly backed away with a sigh. No slow dancing for me.

A throat cleared. I jumped and whipped around to find Chase standing next to me.

He held his hand out like a prince in a romance novel. "I believe this dance is mine."

My stomach flipped. "I believe it is."

I put my hand into his and let him walk me back out onto the dance floor.

I slipped my hand up to his shoulder as my gaze moved to his. His smile grew as he wrapped his arm around my waist, splaying his large hand across the small of my back. Then, he tugged me in just a little closer, until our chests were nearly touching.

I inhaled sharply at the contact. Our eyes were still locked as we began to sway side to side. My vision tunneled to the two of us out on the dance floor, as if we were in a movie and the rest of the cast disappeared. Suddenly just us on the floor while I twirled in my *Beetlejuice* dress with a blond-headed prince who sent shivers down my entire body.

"Wasn't sure you were actually going to dance," I said.

"And miss this?"

"Obviously, it would have been a huge loss for you."

He laughed softly. "I suppose it would have."

He spun me around. I fumbled through the steps and laughed as I nearly crashed back into him.

"A little warning would have been nice."

"Not when I get that smile," he said and then did it again.

My smile was wide as he moved me effortlessly through the steps. I'd never ballroom danced in my life, but he clearly knew what he was doing, and his lead was easy to follow once I let myself relax.

"Where did you learn how to dance like this?" I asked once I was back in his arms again, swaying to the music, my arms around his neck.

"Ah, Junior League," he said with a grimace. "My sister was a debutante, and I took lots of dance lessons."

I could barely contain my laugh. "Junior League is *absurd*."

He nodded. "Tell me about it. I was the one who suffered through it."

"It puts the patriarchy on a pedestal. The entire reason they started was for a woman to enter society and, like, put their virginity on display."

"I'm not defending them. My sister was super into it, but most people like them now to wear the fancy dress and hang out with their friends."

I sighed. That sounded right. No one wanted to be uncomfortable and question why things were the way they were. It was easier to just fit into society than to buck against it. I'd learned that time and time again.

"I will say that the dancing comes in handy at times like this," he said, putting the focus on the way his hand slid across my stomach as he twisted me in place.

He spun me back in and raised an eyebrow, as if to say, *See?*

I leaned into him, running one hand down the front

of his immaculately cut suit. "I learned *very* different dance moves." I waggled my eyebrows. "There were a lot more *window* and *wall* and a lot less appropriate distances."

He actually snorted at that and tugged me in closer. "Is this better?"

My breath caught on the *yes* I wanted to utter.

But instead, I was struck by how handsome he was. I had to tilt my head back to admire his lush lips and the high peaks of his cheekbones and the little dimples that appeared in his cheeks. From here, I could see the flecks of gold in his irises and the scar above his eyebrow. A tiny imperfection on the otherwise perfect face. Somehow, it made me like him even more.

I reached up and brushed a finger against it. "How did you get this?"

His hand captured mine, lacing our fingers together. "I'll trade you my secret for one of your own."

I arched an eyebrow. "Oh, is it a secret?"

"Maybe."

"What would you like in return?" I asked baldly, letting my eyes linger on his lips.

He was stopped from answering by the end of the song. He slowly lowered me into an impressive dip, my long hair trailing behind me on the hardwood floor. Our eyes locked, and for a second, I could imagine what it would be like to have his lips on mine. To see exactly where this song and dance were leading.

Then, he righted me as effortlessly as the dip had started, and we broke apart as the music shifted into a rendition of the Electric Slide.

He slid a hand through his hair, glancing sideways, as if debating on what to do. "It's a little...crowded," he finally said. "Do you want to go for a walk?"

I nodded, finally realizing how many people were staring at us. "Yes."

He grabbed my hand again, and then we were avoiding the bridal party and stepping through a side door, out into the cool spring evening air. Away from the wedding, I felt free. No more eyes on us. Just me and him and a clear night sky.

He hadn't released my hand, and we strolled down the stone path that led out to the vineyards.

"Are you going to tell me about your scar? Since it's such a big secret," I teased.

He ran a finger over it. "I suppose it's not much of a secret," he admitted. "Usually, when people ask about it, I make up some outrageous story. Like I was mauled by a bear or got it while saving someone's life."

I laughed. "And the real story is?"

"I flipped my kayak when I was in middle school and hit a rock. I had to get a ton of stitches. Bled like a bitch. Had the *worst* fear of water for years after that."

"I like the real story," I said, replacing his finger with my own. "It's a battle wound. I have one of those."

When we reached the vineyards, I lifted my skirt at the hem until it was nearly to my hip. There was a knotted scar that had made me hate bikinis all through high school until I decided that was bullshit and I should be proud of it.

"What happened?" Chase dropped onto his heels to get a better look at the scar.

He ran a finger over the skin, and I shivered. When he looked up at me, I had to bite down my desire at the sight of him on his knees before me.

"Ice skating crash." I swallowed at his inspection, heat pooling in all the right places with him so close. "Someone ran into me, the ice went out from under my blades, and..." I clapped my hands together to indicate the crash.

"Shit," he said.

But he hadn't stood up. His hand slid around to the back of my thigh. His face level with my pussy. His eyes examining the lightning-strike scar.

His gaze skirted up to mine. A silent question on his lips. Permission.

I stood there in deep-seated need at the feel of his fingers digging into my thigh and the mirrored look caught in his irises. What was I doing? I'd only known him for a matter of hours. And here he was, on his knees in front of me, and I'd thrown out the entire rule book in his presence. I was a sex-positive type of girl. I always encouraged my girlfriends to have all the fun they wanted. *You're only young once!* But there was giving advice and taking advice.

Was I insane for wanting this? For nodding and giving him the green light?

Permission granted.

His lips quirked upward, and then they were on my scar. His tongue darting out and tracing the line of my hip, where ice had carved a hole out of my skin.

A soft exhale escaped my lips. Not quite a moan, but

fuck, if he'd kissed me anywhere else, I might have come undone right then and there.

His eyes were on mine again as he pulled back. I wasn't sure if I was happy that he hadn't taken more or glad that he hadn't pushed his luck. Because I was pretty sure he was right; luck *was* on his side tonight.

4

CHASE

Well, I was fucking done for.

I'd known that I wanted her before she lifted her skirt up and shown me the scar on her hip. Now, I was certain that I wanted little more than to drive her home right this second. It had been *years* since I'd been this attracted to someone immediately. Actually, maybe it had never happened. There was a spark here that I couldn't name or apparently deny.

As I'd just put my lips on her with nothing more than a nod of agreement. I could barely control my cock straining against my suit pants.

Her eyes were glazed when I came to my feet. I wanted to push my hands up into her hair and claim her lips. No part of me wanted to wait. I hadn't been able to keep from kissing her hip and caressing her thigh. Would I have found her wet if I'd slid up higher?

Fuck.

Fuuuck.

"I...I..." She stammered over her words as she

dropped her skirt. "I don't think anyone has ever looked that close at my scar."

I wouldn't mind getting an even closer look, if I was honest. But I had so many questions for this siren who had wrapped a fist around my heart.

"Well, you offered the perfect view."

She ducked her head and then met my gaze again. "Don't know what compelled me."

"I know that feeling," I admitted.

She swallowed, and something passed between us—a zing of connection that I'd felt the moment our eyes locked at the ceremony. As if neither of us could stop this runaway train now that it was off the tracks.

But I could see that she didn't know what to do with this connection any more than I did. I wanted to go *fast, fast, fast*, but I didn't want to scare her.

"Do you still skate?" I asked to bring the subject back around.

She nodded. "Pretty sure it only made me more relentless."

"I get that. In college, I took up kayaking again to get over my fear. I figured the only way out was through."

"Exactly," she said, gesturing emphatically. "The ice couldn't break me."

"Yes. My friends thought I was nuts, but I still kayak now. I love it. I take my dog, Bowie, out to Buffalo Springs Lake a lot."

She blinked. "Bowie? Like *David* Bowie?"

"Yeah. He's my favorite artist," I said apologetically. "I know it's dated, but..."

"You're joking," she gasped, nearly falling over herself.

"Uh, no?" I said hesitantly.

I never met people who understood the musical merits of David Bowie. He'd raised a generation. He'd been the sexual awakening of men and women alike. He was an *icon*. I would never accept Bowie slander.

"I was *literally* just listening to 'Ziggy Stardust' in the car."

My face went skeptical. "No, you weren't."

"At full blast, mind you. As it is the only way to listen to Bowie."

"I have the records at my house. They sound insane on the Bose stereo system."

"I am dying," she gasped. "I *need* that in my life. My mom sold all of her records from her roadie days, and I'm eternally sad about it."

"Your mom was a roadie?" I asked with a laugh.

"Oh my God, yes. It's hilarious. There're all these pictures of her touring with bands and stuff. It's why West got into music in the first place. And where I got my good taste in music. You can only grow up listening to so much Bowie, Mötley Crüe, Guns N' Roses, and the like before you end up with it them as your faves."

"Yeah, I get that. I'm close with my mom, too. She was addicted to REO Speedwagon, Styx, and Journey when I was growing up. I'd go to concerts with her when my dad was out of town. It was our thing."

"Oh man, I'd kill to go. Mom got all her concerts in during her youth and said she doesn't have eardrums for it anymore." She rolled her eyes. "She's also like, *If I'm not front row in a mosh pit, is it even worth it?*"

I cracked up. "Your mom sounds awesome."

She beamed. "She is. I definitely didn't get this way from my dickhole dad."

"Yeah. Feel that. My dad is...not much of a peach either."

The space between us narrowed again. Who the hell was this girl? Why hadn't she existed in my life before this moment?

I'd started this because we'd had a moment at the wedding and continued when I found out she was Jordan's little sister. But somehow, it had gone beyond that. She was as relentless in her pursuit of things she enjoyed. She loved the same music as me. We had similar family dynamics. And beyond all of that, I felt like I could relax with her. Like I didn't have to second-guess every move the way I had in the past.

Everything felt simple. Effortless.

And I decided to go with the flow. I wanted this. And I didn't want to wait another minute.

I moved into her space, pushing my hand into her hair, tilting her head up to look at me. She inhaled sharply, her lips parting slightly.

"What are you doing?" she whispered.

"I've wanted to kiss you since the our eyes first locked."

Her smile turned Cheshire. "You've already kissed me."

I tugged her even closer, until our chests were pressed together and I could feel the wild beat of her heart. I dipped my head until our lips nearly touched. Our breath mingling in the space.

"Then, I want to taste your lips."

"Please," she whispered.

The plea on her lips did nothing but make me want her even more earnestly.

There was a pause in the universe as we hung suspended. Her eyes fluttering closed and her exhale of anticipation. The tightening of her hands into the lapels of my suit. The light of the moon illuminating her features. Like an ethereal being on the cusp of giving up her immortality for a taste of desire.

My lips bridged the small gap that remained between us. Our mouths fit together, soft and pillowy. She tasted of the cherry aftereffects of her wine. I would never think of cherries again without the thought of this moment.

She gasped against me as my tongue brushed against her, tender and inviting. Her chest heaved and pressed tighter into me. I tilted her up even more so I could dive ever deeper. I wanted to drown in her.

"Oh," she whispered.

We broke apart long enough for her to look up at me with bedroom eyes. As if she'd had a revelation.

I grinned. "Oh?"

"Is that what that's supposed to feel like?"

"You haven't seen anything yet," I told her with all sincerity.

And then we both went under.

Our kiss flipped like a light switch.

My hands tangled harder in her hair. Her hands sought for purchase. Our bodies moved against each other, fervent and desperate. The thread between us snapped taut, and what we'd just been navigating since that first look came to a head. Our tongues collided with need. A dance as much as the ballroom one we'd done inside. Now, we were out here in the dry evening air, and I wanted nothing more than to devour her whole.

If we had been anywhere else, I would have pushed for more. Found a quiet place away from the rest of the world, rucked up her skirt, and found all new ways to make her moan. I wanted it with a fire that I hadn't known existed in me. No one had made me this reckless in my entire life. And, fuck, I was hard enough that I was considering it.

We broke apart then with chest-heaving gasps and wide eyes.

"We should...get out of here."

She touched her lips like I'd burned her. "Yes," she whispered.

I took her hand in mine and brought it to my lips. Her eyes tracked my mouth as I pressed kisses into her knuckles.

"I drove. You could...come home with me."

There was no hesitancy in her expression. She'd felt exactly what I had.

"Okay."

"Yeah?"

She nodded. Then, she blinked, as if returning to the world. "Oh, wait. No. No, I can't go."

My heart lurched at the quick rejection. "Oh."

"No, I want to," she said immediately. "I just...I agreed

to be the designated driver for my brothers. So, I have to drive them home."

"Ah, I see. That is responsible of you."

"Yeah." She chewed on her bottom lip. "Sort of regretting it now."

I laughed. "It's all right."

"Maybe we could meet up tomorrow," she offered hopefully.

"I was going to go kayaking with Bowie tomorrow. You could come."

"Yes," she said, nodding along. "I would *love* to do that. Here, give me your number, and we can make plans."

She offered me her phone, and I added my details. I passed the phone back to her, and she tugged me in close, snapping a picture of us in the moonlight. It was blurry, but she was looking up at me with adoration in her eyes.

"There, now, you have my number."

I pulled my phone out and saw the picture and laughed. "Good. And our picture."

"A memory of our night."

"I don't want the night to be over," I said, tugging her in for another kiss.

She sighed into me. "Me either. But kayaking tomorrow for sure."

I cursed the Wrights for stealing the rest of my night as we headed back up to the wedding. It was easy to blame them for everything at this point. At least we had plans for the next day. Maybe that was for the better. Then, she would see that I didn't just want sex from her. I didn't *just* want sex. Because the way we'd collided in the vineyard made it perfectly clear that I wanted to ravage her all night long.

I let her go in without me since I was still indecent. I needed to calm down before I could reenter the party. That was when I realized…I didn't need to go back.

I'd shown up for my oldest friend.

I'd found something inexplicably better.

The door was closed. I was ready to put it firmly behind me. I'd said my congratulations to Annie already anyway. There was nothing left to say. Time to move on.

So, I walked around the outside of the barn and toward the parking lot. The wedding planner was ushering people around to get them in place for the grand exit. People would probably still party for another hour, but Annie and Jordan were leaving. Another thing I didn't need to say farewell to.

I caught Harley standing with one of her twin brothers, the one in Converse and not a suit—I couldn't otherwise tell them apart. Our eyes locked again, and she shot me a bold smile. I smiled back. Her brother put his hand on her shoulder to stop her, which was my cue to get out of here.

Once I got to my Porsche a few minutes later, I leaned back against the hood. I could see sparklers lighting up the barn. The grand exit had begun. Yet I wasn't thinking about Annie at all. I was wondering if the vivid blonde was having a good time. If she was wishing she were here with me right now, the way I wanted her to be. Was I an idiot for wanting to text her right now and ask to hang out after she dropped off her brothers?

I glanced down at my phone, ignoring Ashleigh's barrage of texts, and pulled up the photo of Harley and me from the vineyard.

Fuck it.

No second-guessing.

I had another thought...let's meet after?

After a few minutes with it on Delivered, but not Read, I sighed and stuffed my phone back into my pocket. She probably wasn't even leaving yet.

I palmed the key to my car, deciding to call it a night, when a figure appeared out of the darkness.

Her eyes lit up. "This is *your* car?"

I glanced down at the outrageous sports car I'd purchased when I opened my own law firm here in town. "Yes."

She laughed. "Of course it is." She gestured to the Kia next to it. "This is mine."

"Where are your brothers?"

Her grin widened as she stepped between my legs. My hands dropped to her hips.

"They are going home with their dates," she told me. "I'm off the hook."

"So, you're free?"

"I'm all yours."

5

HARLEY

I couldn't believe I was doing this.

I'd had every opportunity to walk away, but I hadn't taken them. Hadn't wanted to take them. I wanted to go home with Chase. I'd regret it forever if I didn't see where this was going.

Not that my brothers would see it that way. Well, they didn't know what had happened out in the vineyards. I certainly wasn't going to tell them.

Thankfully, Whitt had left with Eve while I was out. He was more overbearing about that sort of thing. But West had noticed that we'd both disappeared. He'd grabbed me before I left and told me not to even think about it. I'd laughed and told him I was going home. He was going home with Nora. Why should he care?

Of course, I'd thought that I *was* going home when I said that.

I hadn't expected to find Chase sitting on the shiny red Porsche my brothers had been drooling over. Somehow, in the full parking lot, we'd ended up right next to each other. It felt as serendipitous as the rest of the evening. I'd had no choice.

That didn't mean I wasn't a little nervous. Even though we'd clicked immediately. There hadn't been a single moment of nerves when we were together.

This was out of character for me.

I'd dated people in high school. Obviously, I wasn't a virgin. Since that was a concept that I didn't even *believe* in. It was a culture morality norm that had been forced upon us. Nothing changed when we had sex. No way was I going to act like I was *losing* anything. Fuck that.

But...the guys I'd been interested in were always West's and Whitt's friends. Guys who were years older than me.

When I'd been seventeen, it was fine for me to be into the twenty-three-year-old guys who hung out with my brothers of the same age. But none of them had ever acted on it.

And it was impossible for me, after all that time with older guys, to look at the guys my age and not see dumb, drooling Neanderthals. Boys my age were unsupervised toddlers. I couldn't deal with any of their stupidity.

Chase was *nothing* like those guys.

He was fun and funny. He had good taste in music. A fucking insane car. He wasn't afraid to ask for what he wanted. Even when I'd had to reject him, he hadn't been all butthurt, like guys my age. He'd just asked for more time. Time I wanted to give to him. Time I wanted to use to see where this was going.

But I was glad that I had my car, just in case.

I parked it out front of his house on the north side of town.

And by house, I meant *mansion*.

I should have expected it when we drove into Rush. It was a neighborhood that had been around since the '50s, and all the huge houses had been gutted and totally renovated from top to bottom. I'd gone with friends to a party over here, and I still couldn't believe that they weren't all worth a million dollars or more. In Seattle, these houses would have gone for eight figures, easy.

His house was absolutely one of them. The place was fucking enormous. It had a three-car garage with exterior lighting, immaculate landscaping, and aged oaks in the front yard. I couldn't even imagine what it looked like on the inside. I still wasn't used to everything in Texas being bigger.

Chase pulled his Porsche into one of the garage spaces and waited for me as I grabbed my purse and headed up the driveway. He pocketed his keys and straightened his suit as I approached.

"Nice place," I said.

He shrugged. "Thanks. That's what happens when your family is in real estate."

He pulled open the door through the garage and let me step in first. He flipped the light on, and I barely kept my jaw from hitting the floor. My brother's houses were pretty impressive, all things considered, but this was something else entirely. This was sleek and sophisticated with dark wood beams, coordinated furniture that fit but wasn't too matchy-matchy, and an entire *wall* of records.

"Wow," I muttered. "This is great."

"Thanks. I've collected most of the pieces from antique stores over the years. My mom kept insisting I needed a design to bring it all together, and I only relented when she worked with a local company that refurbished antique pieces."

"Juxtaposh?" I guessed.

He nodded. "You've been?"

"It's the coolest place in town. She did a great job."

"Yeah. I think the pièce de résistance is the record display." He gestured to the far wall. "Take your pick. I'm going to let Bowie out."

I strode across the room and examined the records. His favorites were in little slots on the wall with their covers facing outward. I saw The Beatles' *White Album*, Bowie's *The Rise and Fall of Ziggy Stardust and the Spiders from Mars*, Queen's , Pink Floyd's classic *The Dark Side of the Moon*, and even Nirvana's *Nevermind*. As I fingered through the individual records in alphabetized containers for the rest of his immense collection, I found Led Zeppelin, Radiohead, Bruce Springsteen, AC/DC, Jimi Hendrix, and so many more.

I itched to take out each beautiful vinyl, lie on the floor, and listen for the next several days. There were so many classics here. My jealousy was primal and intense. I wanted all of them. Damn my mom for getting rid of her collection.

I was trailing my finger down the edge of The Doors self-titled album when a bark jolted me. I barely turned in time to find a frolicking golden retriever bounding toward me.

"Oh my goodness," I gasped, dropping onto my heels. "Hello there, buddy."

Bowie jumped up, putting both paws on my shoulders. I laughed, nearly toppling over from his enthusiasm.

"Bowie, down."

"He's fine," I insisted.

But Bowie leaped back, running zoomies around the living room before colliding with Chase's legs and nearly taking him out. Chase laughed and ruffled his ears.

"You mangy thing."

Bowie responded by jumping to his feet and licking Chase from jaw to temple.

"God, Bowie, we need to teach you about consent." He'd removed his suit jacket, and he used the sleeve of his white button-up to wipe off the slobber.

"Do dogs understand the concept of consent?"

Chase gestured to Bowie, who raced across the room and into my arms. "Not this dog."

"Well, it's fine," I said, scratching his ears. "You're such a good boy, aren't you? The goodest boy."

His tongue lolled out, and he leaned his head into my hand. I was already in love. I'd always wanted a dog, but Mom was a cat person, and we'd grown up with a tabby that hated me. It was a mutual feeling. Mom had sworn that since I wanted to exist in a Halloween movie, I should like cats, but alas, it was not to be.

"How long have you had him?"

"Just a year. That's why he still has puppy energy. My sister's friend had a litter, and she convinced me to take one."

"Good choice."

"Yeah," he said with a head shake at his dog, who had just rolled over and given me his belly to scratch. "He's fun, and he loves the water, so that's a bonus. But he never took much to all the training he had. He'll do it, but on his own terms."

"That seems fair," I said as I came to my feet. "I don't take orders well either."

Chase laughed. "I'll keep that in mind."

My face flushed as our eyes met across the room. Well, I hadn't meant it like *that*.

Chase just grinned at the color on my cheeks and patted his leg twice. "Okay, bud, let's go outside."

Bowie bounded toward him, and they headed toward the back door. I returned my attention to the records and tried to get my face to return to normal. I didn't know how he flustered me so easily. I wasn't the kind of girl who got like this about a guy, and yet Chase did it for me.

A few minutes later, he appeared at my side and held out a glass with amber liquid in it. "Hope whiskey is okay. My wine collection isn't anywhere as good as my records."

I took the drink from his hand. "Whiskey is fine." I sipped the drink as I rummaged more through the collection. "I have intense jealousy over this."

"Yeah? Which one should we listen to?"

"You pick. I listen to literally all of this." My hand hovered over a copy of the Eagles' *Hotel California*. My dad's favorite. I shivered and pushed past it. "What are you feeling?"

"All right. Might as well go for the classic."

He pulled Ziggy Stardust off of its place of honor and removed the vinyl from the sleeve. He set the vinyl on the track and started the player. I watched the needle rise and lower itself, a soft scratching noise the only sound as Chase flipped on the Bose speaker system.

"Battery at sixty percent. Connected to Chase's iPhone and ATVT," the speaker proclaimed.

The David Bowie album was spinning on the turntable, but what came out of the speaker was anything but the lyrical genius. Instead, blasting at full volume was none other than ABBA's "Dancing Queen."

"What the fuck?" Chase said.

I couldn't stop myself; I burst into laughter. He was pawing frantically at the speaker, but the dance pop lyrics just continued to serenade us from the speakers. Finally, he glanced over at me and also burst into laughter.

"You like ABBA?"

"What?" he asked, losing all his bravado. "Don't you? This song is a bop."

I snorted. "Did you just call 'Dancing Queen' a bop?"

He shrugged and ran with it, grabbing my hands and forcing me to dance dramatically around his living room. The laughter was entirely contagious, and as we bounced and twirled on the hardwood floor, we couldn't keep the giant smiles off our faces. When the chorus hit, I gave in to his antics and began to sing along with the tune.

"I knew you liked it," he said.

"It's not my go-to, but it's a classic."

I did a little shimmy as I sang about dancing and royalty and the joy of being seventeen and free. It felt a little more realistic here, with him, like this. How young and reckless I was being and how, in the blink of an eye, it all slipped away. And it was just us enjoying this song and each other without inhibitions.

At the final round of the chorus, Chase lifted me up into the air. I giggled as I raised my hands and let him spin me in a circle. Whatever had come over us, I was living for it. Letting the night take us wherever it might.

Then, the song came to an end, and he slowly lowered me to the ground, my chest sliding against his all the way down. Our eyes locked as I passed from above him to below his very kissable lips.

All the air left the room. I wasn't sure if another song even played after ABBA. All thoughts of setting the record player up and listening all weekend evaporated. I knew exactly what my preference would be.

Right here.

Right now.

With Chase's hands on me.

I looked up at him through my lashes when my feet finally touched the ground.

But he was still moving toward me, his hands cupping my jaw and lifting my lips to his. And I could do nothing but let him.

6

HARLEY

The world shifted as Chase devoured me in one perfect kiss. He tipped my head back for better access and slipped his hands down my back to pull our bodies closer together.

It felt like I'd been waiting for this moment all my life.

This was like waking up to a perfect spring morning.

It was like ice cream on a hot day.

It was like winning front-row tickets to see your favorite artist.

My heart was beating so fast, practically out of my chest. My breathing was heavy. And my hands were frantic, trying to feel every inch of him.

I needed more. I wanted his skin against mine. I wanted his heart beating in time with mine. And I needed us both panting and breathless.

"Fuck," he growled against my mouth. "Whiskey tastes good on you."

I huffed out a breath. "Want to taste more?" The

words rushed out of my mouth before I could stop them. And yet I couldn't keep the coquettish smile off of my face.

I wasn't ashamed to ask what I wanted from him. He'd made it abundantly clear that was what he was offering. He'd knelt before me in the vineyard with my scarred hip in his hand and placed a kiss along the line.

And that had sealed it for me.

It had begun long before that. With the smirk on his lips when he caught me looking, the swipe of a napkin against the drop of red wine I'd spilled when we nearly collided, the offered dance. The dance itself had been the game leading here. His hands on the small of my back, the exposed column of my neck, the mirrored look in our eyes when he righted me and we both knew we couldn't spend another minute in a crowded room.

"I want to taste all of you, Harley."

He stepped toward me, an opening dance that he was once again leading, and I followed, retreating in the wake of the predator. My heart beat a staccato against my throat as he neared. The desire palpable in the dim lighting.

My back hit the wall, and air whooshed out of my lungs in surprise. There he was, looming over me, his hands going to either side of my face as he stared down at me, as if he planned to learn every single exhalation from my lips.

"Would you like that?" he asked as his hands slid over my shoulders to find my wrists.

"Would I like...what?" I asked, already delirious with desire.

"For me to taste you." He pushed my hands above my head.

"Yes," I squeaked, losing all my cool as he pressed my wrists together and held the delicate things with one of his hands.

"Where exactly should I begin?" he teased.

He ducked his head into my neck and kissed where it met my collarbone. I groaned at the sensitive skin, squirming against the wall, where he held me securely. He kissed his way up my neck slowly, torturously, until he brushed his nose behind my earlobe.

"Here?" he asked.

"I…"

But no more words followed. He drew the lobe into his mouth and flicked his tongue against it. I tried to free my wrists as sensation rushed up my body, but he just tightened his grip, holding me in place.

"Not there?"

"Uh…well…"

His fingers were drawing a trail down my sternum and then between my breasts. A soft gasp left my throat, and he smirked, knowing precisely the effect he had on me. He slid his fingers under my breast, sparking heat with every movement. He found my nipple through the thin material of my black dress. I'd opted out of a bra and could feel every sensation, like his fingers were against bare skin.

His mouth came to the front of my dress, hot air blowing against the pebbled nipple.

"Oh," I whispered.

"Hmm," he said.

"Hmm?" I asked, my eyes opening to a slit in confusion.

"Going to have to get you out of this dress to taste these."

He drew a finger around the other nipple until it hardened. I squirmed harder against him. Heat built in my core, and I could feel the wetness soaking into my panties.

"Perhaps later then," he decided as if he'd been debating.

"Oh," I said with a pout.

He chuckled, leaning forward and nipping at my bottom lip that had popped out. "Later is a promise."

Then, he released my wrists, dropped to a knee before me, and rucked up my skirt. He hiked my leg up over his shoulder and met my heated gaze with one of his own, a lascivious grin spreading across his lips.

"What about here?" His lips pressed to my inner thigh. "Or here?" He moved upward. "Or here? Is this what you want me to taste?" he asked, leaving a trail of kisses in his wake.

I huffed. "A little higher."

His eyes snapped up to mine and stayed there as his fingers inched higher, running along the lacy material of my thong. Another gasp left my mouth, but I was still trained on his eyes, and he could see every single reaction that crossed my face.

"Right...right there," I told him.

His grin was feral. "You're wet."

"Yes."

"For me."

I nodded, biting down on my lip.

He hooked a finger under the edge of my panties and pushed them to the side before sliding his finger down the seam of my pussy. My eyes rolled into the back of my head as I moaned.

"Fuck," he ground out. "That's so fucking hot."

Then, he slipped his finger inside of me. My legs quivered at the contact, my body contracting at the first feel of him. Oh, how I wanted more, more, more. One finger was sweet torture with how hot my body was already for him. Oh God!

He pulled out and inserted a second finger. I tipped my head back, reveling in the feeling. Wanting more, needing this, holding on to the climax that was building as I pulsed around his fingers. I was so fucking turned on that I didn't know how long I could hold out.

This had never been a problem in my life. I could get myself off. I could even sometimes come from oral or sex, but the conditions had to be perfect. And—let's be honest—the conditions were rarely perfect.

And yet I was close enough that if he thrummed my clit, I might come undone in a matter of minutes.

"This isn't what I want," he said, pulling out.

"I...wait," I gasped. "I was..."

But he grinned at me as he lifted me up, wrapping my legs around his waist, and carried me to the chair. I protested as he set me on my feet, but he still had that smirk on his lips. The one that said he was in charge here.

I wanted to put my foot down, but he was already turning me around to face the arm of the chair. Then, without preamble, he bent me forward at the waist. I gasped as he threw the floof of my skirt up out of the way, yanked my panties to the ground, and promptly buried his face into my pussy.

"Oh fuck!"

But there wasn't time for any more words as he slid his fingers back through my wet folds and his tongue lapped against the sensitive bud of my clit. And I had my ass in the air with his arm banded over my hips and nowhere to go but through.

I couldn't even squirm away from the intense sensations rushing through me. I didn't *want* to escape, and yet I needed to so desperately. From my fingers to my toes and everywhere in between, my nerves were sparking to life. My orgasm was held back by a string.

When he changed from lapping to a direct flick against my clit, there was nothing I could do but unleash.

I cried out into the stillness of the living room. My head buried into a pillow. My fingers clenching down on the soft brown leather. Pussy spasming against his lips, their own undoing.

Everything went suddenly silent. Like I'd entered another dimension, where this incredible, indescribable feeling had a name more fitting than *orgasm*. It had to be more than that. I'd come before. I'd used my own fingers to bring myself to climax. Whatever words you wanted to use for it, they were not the words to describe what had just happened.

I felt like I'd dropped bodily through the floor into a demon dimension, where he'd sucked the life out of me and left me spent. Better yet, I wanted to remain wherever the hell he'd left me. A defenseless, mewling little thing, desperate for more of what he was offering.

Chase slowly extracted his fingers and planted a kiss on my ass. "That was perfect."

I slid backward off of the chair and onto the floor, pooling into a boneless puddle. "It was."

He disappeared into the kitchen. I heard running water, and then he returned to stand over me. His cock bulged against his suit pants, and oh, how I wanted to have *my* fill of him now. Unfortunately, I physically could not move.

"You seem content," he admitted.

"I think you broke me."

He laughed, an easy, pleased smile staying on his face. "I sure hope not. I have more plans for you."

"Oh yeah?"

"Plans to fuck you."

"I like these plans."

He chuckled as he lifted me to my feet. My legs could barely hold me. He caught me in his grip. Then, without a second thought, he lifted me bodily over his shoulder like I was a rag doll.

"Oof," I gasped.

But he was already walking, unconcerned with the fact that he was manhandling me. Something I never could have conceived allowing before this moment. Maybe it was a time and place thing. Because in this time and place, I'd do anything for him to leave me weightless and call me perfect again.

He carried me down a short hallway, toeing open a tall door. He flipped the lights on and tossed me down onto the softest bed I'd ever been on in my life. His bedroom was massive. The kind of thing that was the size of many Seattle apartments. Twice the size of my dorm room. It had the same aesthetic as the living room—antique chic. The bed was refurbished hard wood, the comforter the softest bluest cotton, with floor-to-ceiling curtains, a navy area rug, and a little reading nook with an overstuffed chair and a ten-books-deep TBR pile.

It was both nothing like and exactly like what I'd imagined his room would look like. Masculine, but not a stupid bachelor pad.

And he wasn't just standing in it; he owned it.

He was slowly unbuttoning the cuffs of his white button-up, and then starting at the top, he revealed inch after glorious inch of tan, toned chest. He was the kind of man who must have spent considerable time in the gym. Or else he was just a god. There was no other explanation for those abs.

My mouth salivated at the sight. I'd been too gooey to do anything about it before, but I wanted nothing more than to run my hands all over him now.

I sat up in bed and tugged him forward by his belt. He released the last button of his shirt and stopped to watch me with a soft laugh.

"You're not the only one who gets to have fun," I told him.

"I was under the impression that you were having a good time." He arched an eyebrow. "Or did I misinterpret how hard I just made you come?"

My cheeks flushed. "No misinterpretation," I confessed. "But I want to play, too."

"By all means," he agreed with a small smile playing on his lips.

I drew him another step closer, bringing his thighs fully between my spread legs. I slid one hand along the top of his suit pants. He inhaled sharply at the move, but didn't stop me. My hands ran over the hard contour of his six-pack to the firm planes of his chest. He was...solid.

A fact that only made me wonder how *solid* he was elsewhere.

I was definitely going to find out.

I leaned in, pressing a kiss directly above his belly button.

Another sharp inhale.

Oh, I liked that.

I glanced up to find him watching me, unmoving. As if he was barely restraining himself. A caged animal lurked underneath, and I was toying with him, like, *Here, kitty, kitty*.

My fingers went to his belt, carefully undoing the clasp and sliding it out of the belt loops. I tossed it unceremoniously onto the floor, popped the button, and dragged the zipper down to the base. His cock strained against the fabric, and a small thrill ran through me that *I* was what had caused this. He wanted *me*, and by the dark gleam in his eye, he wanted me desperately.

I nearly had to cross my legs at the thought. Fuck.

With our eyes still connected, I drew a black-painted nail down the length of him. He bucked into my hand, and I grinned.

"Are you just going to play with it?" he asked.

"No," I told him, mischief in my voice. "I have other

plans."

My hand slid into his boxers and circled the head, sliding down, down, down to the base. My eyes widened in shock. And his satisfied look was pure delight. He liked my shock. He liked it *a lot.*

He was...big.

BIG.

I didn't understand how pants contained him. How anything contained him. I certainly didn't know how *I* was going to contain him. In fact, I was having second thoughts about how exactly this was going to be possible.

"You said you had other plans." His hand came up to cup my jaw, and he brushed a finger across my dark red bottom lip. "Are you going to tease me, or are you going to suck my cock?"

"What if I'm a cocktease?" I asked, squirming at the mere thought.

His eyes went dark and hooded. "Then, it's only fair that I edge your next orgasm the rest of the night."

My mouth popped open, and he stuck his thumb inside before I could utter a word.

"Yes. Just like that, baby girl."

I closed my mouth around his thumb, teasing the tip with my tongue. I'd given plenty of head before. I actually enjoyed it. But now, I was debating whether or not him edging me all night would be a punishment or a privilege.

Hmm.

He didn't give me much of an option as his pants dropped to the floor and he replaced his thumb with his cock. I opened wider to accommodate him, and still, it was a stretch on my jaw. My hands went to his hips, and I bobbed forward and back on his length. Well, as much of him as I could fit in my mouth. But what I couldn't, I made up for with my hand on the shaft and unbridled enthusiasm for the task. I wanted him to come hard enough that he also turned into a fucking puddle on the ground.

"Fuck," he growled, his hands moving into my long blonde locks. "Fuck yes, baby girl, just like that. Fuck, your mouth feels so good. So hot and wet. You're making me so hard that I'm not going to be able to hold on."

His words only drove me forward. Heating me up just as much as he was. Somehow, he lengthened more as he throbbed inside my mouth. A desperation took over as he was barely able to hold himself back.

Just as I felt he was near the edge, I slipped a hand to his balls and massaged them. He grunted, thrusting deep into my throat. Hard enough to make me gag, but then he was coming, hot and salty into the back of my throat. I could do nothing but swallow him down. My eyes were watering as he retreated, and he ran his thumb over an unshed tear.

"Perfect," he told me, adoration in those eyes. "I'm going to need that pussy now."

And I was shocked to see he'd lost none of his hardness from the orgasm. It was still long, thick, and veiny, now pointing upward.

He stepped over to a side table, removed a condom, and slid it onto his impressive length. I took the time to pull the side zipper on my dress and shuck the garment onto the floor.

When he turned back around, he widened his eyes, hand on his cock, pumping once, twice.

"Jesus fucking Christ," he groaned.

I felt the same. With his pants discarded, I could see his powerful thighs and his tight ass and every corded muscle in between. I'd never been so turned on just from looking at someone.

"Come here," he commanded.

I came to my feet, all shyness evaporating in the wake of his adoring gaze. I slunk toward him, my breasts hanging heavy, nipples pert. His hands slid to my waist, and he drew me against him. His cock was hard against my stomach between us as his lips descended, and I tasted our mingled arousal on our tongues.

He pressed me back into the bed, yanking my ass until it was nearly off of the bed and spreading my legs wide so he got a full view of my wet pussy. I was glad for the years of ice skating so that I was limber enough to hold the pose.

Then, our bodies met as he aligned his cock with my opening. Grasping my hand in his and pressing it hard back into the mattress, he thrust home.

I cried out at the full length of him plowing deep inside of me. He smothered my cry with a kiss before retreating, placing a steadying hand on my stomach, and then pulling out. It felt just as fucking good on the way out before he slammed back in. My back jerked upward on the mattress with every blow, and I was seeing stars as we united over and over again.

"So close," I gasped.

His thumb came to my clit, circling it round and

round as he continued to ram into me. I was barely coherent as my body built and built and built to a crescendo. I reached for him, wanting to feel his skin against mine, but he was relentless, drawing out my pleasure until I believed to my core that he really would edge me all night before letting me have another orgasm. And I would like it.

"Come for me," he said.

With one more thrust, I crashed into a million pieces. I screamed into the room, tightening all around him. He only lasted another minute, thrusting harder and faster through my orgasm before he bottomed out inside of me, coming with a roar.

It was primal, feral, and fucking hot as hell to watch his head tip back and his mouth widen. To see the haze of satisfied desire in his blue eyes. And to see contentment cascade over him as he finished and slumped forward over me.

He pressed our foreheads together, and nothing in the world had ever felt so right. We were naked and sweaty and panting. And still, I wanted him.

"More," was my only plea.

He startled, pulling back far enough to make sure he'd heard me right. "You want more?"

"Yes," I said.

"You're sure?"

My hand came to his cheek. "I could never get enough of you."

"Then, more you shall have."

And the rest of the night disappeared in a haze of orgasm-laced euphoria. A night I'd never ever forget.

7

CHASE

Harley was sprawled naked beside me when I woke up.

Her blonde hair an unruly halo around her head. Her ass against my hips, stirring my cock. Her hand reaching for mine to band across her bare chest and over those perfect pink nipples.

We'd fucked over and over again last night. And already, I wanted her again. I was insatiable. Ravenous for her. The taste of her skin. The feel of her hair. The pulse of her pussy.

And every soft moment in between when we'd hung out with Bowie, taken a shower, and then crawled into bed to recover. When we'd discussed the finer points of David Bowie's music collection or how Halloween was both of our favorite holiday or the handful of books we were in the middle of—fantasy for me and preferred smut for her, a topic that I could get behind. A delirious litany of things we had in common, places we wanted to go, things we wanted to do, bucket lists we wanted to check off. Still more sex.

She was like a drug that I wasn't sure I would ever get enough of.

I released her hand and slipped my hand down her side, over her hip, and down the soft plane of her leg. I'd kissed every inch of her body last night. I'd mapped it with my hands and tongue and cock. And I wanted to do it all over again.

I moved to the V between her legs. My finger strummed playfully against her clit. Nothing too intense. Just enough to wake her body up.

"Mmm," she murmured, spreading her legs wider.

"Fuck," I muttered as she arched into my hand.

I caught the sight of her pretty pink pussy. A sheen of slickness already ready and waiting for me. My cock lengthened against her back as I dipped my finger down into her wetness and dragged it back up to her clit.

"Oh, mmm," she moaned in her sleep.

She bucked her hips backward, her fingers fisting into the mattress.

All I wanted to do was slide into her sweetness and make her come all over my cock, but I would wait out her orgasm. We had all day after all. I had nowhere to be until Monday morning, when I had to be at the office.

Harley rolled over, her eyes fluttering open. Her mouth popped wide in surprise, and I used that moment to slide two fingers into her waiting pussy.

"Good morning."

Her mouth opened wider. "Oh. Oh fuck," she gasped. "You...I...oh!"

"You were wet when I started. Were you dreaming about me?"

Her cheeks flushed. "Maybe."

"And what was I doing?"

She squirmed under my touch. Her chest rising and falling faster. "You were fucking me."

"Didn't get enough of me last night?"

"I told you I wouldn't get enough of you."

"So you did." I picked up my pace. "And *how* was I fucking you?"

She flushed deeper. "We were...oh!" Her eyes snapped shut, and she tilted her head back. "At...the...lake."

I grinned, planting a kiss on her lips. "I was going to go to the lake with Bowie today."

"Yes...yes," she whispered. "Fuck, Chase, I'm so close."

I slowed down. I hadn't been lying when I said I wanted to hold her orgasms out longer and longer so that I could make them more intense. She whimpered at my pull back though. She really *had* been close. Fuck, she was greedy in all the best ways.

"Not...fair," she forced out.

"Go to the lake with me, and you can show me what we were doing."

"Make me come, and maybe I will."

I laughed softly and slowed even further. "Maybe I'll make you wait until we get there."

"You wouldn't dare."

"Wouldn't I?" I asked, flicking against her clit and making her back bow.

Her eyes opened to slits. "I...I don't have clothes. I'd have to go home to change. I'd need an orgasm before I left, right?" It was more of a plea than a statement.

I pursed my lips. I hadn't thought of that. I didn't want her to go without me. "I don't want you to leave."

"I don't *want* to leave. Right now, I'd like to come."

I kept her right at the edge. "But I do want to fuck you at the lake now."

She laughed softly, a brittle thing. "I could be...quick. Just long enough to pack some clothes and be back."

I pressed a kiss to her lips. "If you must."

"Chase," she pleaded. "Please..."

Then, I smirked and removed my fingers. She groaned.

"But...but..."

I leaned forward and flicked my tongue against her clit. Oh, how I wanted to make her come. Finish us both off. But I wanted her to come back sooner rather than later. Give her some incentive to hurry back.

"I'll finish you off when you get back."

Her mouth dropped open. "That is *not* fair."

"I'll make it worth it," I assured her.

"I could just masturbate," she said as her hand ran down her chest toward her waiting pussy.

I snatched her hand before she could reach the sensitive bud. "Don't you dare."

Her eyes were wide with desire as I held her wrist in a vise grip.

"You don't want to watch me masturbate?" she teased.

"I want to watch," I assured her. "I want it all."

"Then..." She wiggled her fingers.

"Every orgasm you get belongs to me."

Her eyes widened again. I could practically see the cogs working in her brain. As if she wasn't sure how to reconcile her feminism with how much she enjoyed me telling her what to do. She'd told me last night that she would hit anyone who called her baby girl, and yet when I used the name, it'd opened the floodgates. We were a set match because everything she did turned me on, too.

"Fine," she finally relented. "I will *hurry back*. While you torture me."

I laughed as she rolled off the bed, squeezing her legs together briefly before going in search of her discarded clothing. She pulled her dress back over her head as I pulled on a pair of boxers.

"Any idea where my underwear went?"

"Yep," I told her.

She arched an eyebrow. "Well?"

"I might have pocketed them last night."

She toed my suit pants, but I snatched them off the ground.

Her eyes narrowed, and then she held her hand out. "Give me my underwear."

I grabbed her arm and pulled her into me. My lips descended on hers. "I'm keeping them as a souvenir."

"What?" she muttered. "Like you went to a theme park?"

I smirked. "If that's what you want to call it."

She pushed at me with a laugh. "You're filthy."

"I just want to imagine you walking around commando, knowing exactly what I did to this pussy." I slid a hand underneath her skirt. "Exactly what I'm going to do to it later."

"Oh," she whispered. "Well...I don't think I'm going to forget anytime soon."

Still, she tried to reach for her underwear, and I pulled it back.

"Hurry back soon," I said, smacking her on the ass.

She made a sound between disgruntled and horny. "I'm going to make you pay for this."

"I look forward to it, baby girl."

Then, I kissed her one more time. She grabbed her purse and hustled out of the house. It suddenly felt... empty without her.

There was Bowie. But even he sniffed around the house, as if wondering where Harley had gone off to. His new best friend.

"I know, buddy," I said, ruffling his fur as we headed into the kitchen. "I miss her already, too."

Despite giving all the incentive she needed to rush back, I had a feeling it would take her a while to return. Not because I was concerned that she'd change her mind, but just because she probably needed time to process.

So, I took Bowie for a short walk around the block, hopped in a quick shower to wash the layers of sex off of my skin, and then made myself a breakfast sandwich. As I sat down to eat it, I checked my phone to see if Harley had texted.

No luck.

But I had a ridiculous amount from my sister.

I scrolled through a couple of them before rolling my

eyes and giving up, shooting her a text to let her know that, yes, I was alive.

I tossed the phone back onto the counter, finished my sandwich, and went about getting ready for our kayaking trip. I was in the garage, attaching my kayak to the top of my Subaru Forester, when I heard Bowie barking from inside.

A smile came to my face. That must be Harley.

I headed back inside, only to find my dog not with the girl I'd been daydreaming about, but with my sister.

"Ashleigh, what are you doing here?"

She scooted her toe at Bowie. "You still haven't trained it to not jump on people."

"First of all, his name is Bowie. You can use his name. And second, he's still a puppy." I laughed as she tried to scoot away from him and he jumped on her again.

"See!" she said.

"Also, running away from him is only going to make him more playful."

She narrowed her eyes at me. "You're insufferable."

"You were the one who got me the dog," I reminded her.

"Yeah, but I didn't think you'd let him jump on me."

"He's a dog, Ash. What did you expect?" I shook my head at my prim and proper sister.

She was in a beige Chanel suit with pink heels and had clearly had a fresh blowout for her shoulder-length blonde hair that was parted perfectly down the middle. Not a hair out of place.

"What are you doing here anyway? And how did you get in?"

She sidestepped Bowie. "I made a copy of your key."

I sighed heavily through my nose. God, if that wasn't the epitome of my family. "Lovely. Guess I'm having the locks changed."

"You're too lazy to do it," she said, unbothered by my threat. "Anyway, I'm here to discuss the wedding."

She plopped onto my leather couch. The one where I'd gone down on Harley the night before. A smirk came to my lips at the memory.

"What? Why do you look like that?"

"Nothing. I don't want to talk about the wedding."

"But I saw her dress!" Ashleigh said, pulling up her phone. She shoved it toward me. "How gawdy. If she'd married you, I would have picked out something way better. And these bridesmaids dresses." She gagged.

"She wasn't going to marry me," I said with a shake of my head. "And her dress was perfect. You're just being catty."

Ashleigh reared back, pulling her phone to her chest. "Well, *excuse me*. Since when did *you* get over Annie Donoghue?"

Last night.

Well, no, that wasn't true. It had been puttering out for years. Ever since she'd started dating Jordan. But it was last night when I realized that I'd been hanging on to nothing. Neither of us wanted it. Neither of us had ever really stood a chance. And it was better this way.

"A long time ago," I told her. "I don't want to bitch about the wedding. And I have plans, so if that's all you're here for, you should go."

"Plans?" she asked with a raised eyebrow.

"Yeah. I'm going kayaking."

I almost mentioned Harley, but fuck if I wanted to keep this all to myself. The last thing—and I mean, the very last thing I needed—was my obnoxious sister getting her claws into the girl of my dreams.

"Boring." She looked down at her manicure. "All of that time outside. Tans are so early 2000s, brother of mine."

"Sure," I said with a headshake as she came to her feet. "Thanks for letting me know."

"Make sure you wear sunscreen, okay?"

"I will wear sunscreen."

She was nearly to the door when she turned back around. "But, like, did Julian look happy?"

It took everything in me not to roll my eyes.

Julian and Ashleigh had dated for two years before she fucked it up royally. It was one of the many reasons that Wrights and Sinclairs didn't socialize. Another reason not to tell Ashleigh about the Wright who had spent all night in my bed.

"He was with Jennifer," I told her.

She wrinkled her nose. "Yeah. Gross." She sighed again. "Did anything interesting happen at all? You can tell me, you know."

My sister, the queen of gossip.

Hmm, the queen of gossip might actually know something about the Wrights that I didn't since I'd distanced myself.

"I met the new Wrights who'd moved here from Seattle. The ones who were a secret family."

"Old news," she said with a hand wave. "I can't believe you hadn't met them before this."

I shrugged. "We don't run in the same circles."

"Of course not. Weston is a musician. Whitton works for Wright Construction. And the youngest—what's her name? Harley—she is in college at Tech."

I sputtered out an, "Excuse me?"

She tilted her head. "What?"

"She's at Tech?"

"Yeah?" she said like I was an idiot. "That's why Whitton moved with her. She got a full ride and started last semester as a freshman."

Ashleigh continued detailing everything she'd gleaned from her sleuthing of the family, but I didn't hear any of it.

The one word was ringing in my ears.

Freshman.

Harley...couldn't be a freshman.

That...that wasn't even remotely possible.

That would make her...eighteen? Nineteen?

But she...

She...

Fuck.

She'd been drinking. She knew more about wine than me. She'd been wild in bed, asking for exactly what she wanted. She had similar tastes and hopes and dreams as me. I just...could not compute.

"Chase?" Ashleigh asked with narrowed eyes. "Are you okay?"

I cleared my throat. "Yeah. Totally fine."

Lie.

I was frozen.

This was not happening.

I'd known she was young, but not *that* young.

What the fuck was I going to do? Because I could *not* date a fucking teenager. Not even one that was perfect for me.

8

HARLEY

Erika was still asleep in her bunk when I got back into my dorm in the dress I'd worn to the wedding. She rolled over when I flicked on a side light and cracked an eye open.

"Well, well, well," my roommate said, "look who is doing the walk of shame after all the shit you give me?"

"I have no shame about my late night..."

"Early morning," Erika countered.

"I have no shame about what happened," I told her with a grin.

Then, I snatched a spare towel and grabbed a fresh change of clothes.

"Well, what's his name?" Erika tilted her head. "Or her?"

"I think you have a lock on all the girls in our dorm, Erika."

Erika grinned, pulling her bright pink comforter tighter around her. "Yeah, yeah. Well, what can I say? I'm prolific."

"And I think you should do whomever you want."

"You still haven't told me his name."

I laughed. "Chase."

She brought her thumbnail to her mouth and chewed on it. "I don't know a Chase. Is he in our year?"

"Not exactly," I said.

He wasn't in any year. He was definitely not hanging out on Tech's campus at all. None of that had mattered or come up last night. Not when every single other thing in our lives seemed to fit together so well.

"Older?"

"I'm taking a shower!"

"A senior?" Erika begged.

I laughed and then hustled out of the room. After a good long shower, I blew out my long blonde hair and then slicked it up into a ponytail. I didn't need to be showy on a kayak.

A smile came to my face when I thought about returning to his house. God, I hadn't ever wanted to leave. I wanted to stay in the little bubble we'd made, where no one else in the entire world existed. Could I live there forever?

I headed back to my room to find Erika playing video games with her latest fling on the headset. I waved my purse at her to say good-bye.

"No, no, no. Tell me about the guy."

"We're going kayaking. I'll tell you when I get back."

"Second date after the first day! Whoa, Harley-Davidson. That is serious."

I shrugged. "I'm not the one who is afraid of serious."

Erika flipped me off, and we both laughed. "What happened to *I'm too busy to date*? I've tried to set you up."

"Yeah, well, Chase is different."

Erika guffawed. "Good luck with that. I'd date men if men weren't...men. They're never different."

And still I hung on to that place in my heart that said Chase was. The place where he'd called me his baby girl and things felt too coincidental, too perfect, too right. I didn't care what Erika said. I'd be a fool not to see where this was headed.

I slung my bag over my shoulder and traipsed back through the dorm out to my Kia. The sun was as shiny as ever, not a trace of spring showers in sight. And for Lubbock, not a trace of spring dust storms either. The real bane of West Texas's existence. It'd be a glorious day out on the water. I'd never been kayaking before, but I was a quick learner and always up for a new challenge.

The drive to his place was only a matter of minutes north of campus. I parked in the driveway and practically skipped to the front door. I knocked twice, still humming the words to Queen's "Don't Stop Me Now."

The door opened, and Chase appeared in all of his glory. My sigh of relief at the sight of him was audible. I hadn't even meant for it to release. But I felt so much better in his presence. This wasn't even about the fact that he'd held back my orgasm this morning. It'd been hot as fuck, and I knew he'd deliver later. It was just...him.

"Hey," he said, a slight hitch in his voice.

"Hey!" I traipsed inside.

Bowie bounded across the room, and I bent down to let him lick my face.

"Yes, I missed you, too. What a good boy. Yes, so, so cute."

Bowie lapped it all up, rolling onto his back and letting me rub his belly. I laughed, obliging his demands.

Chase had closed the door, but he hadn't said anything, and when I turned back to smile at him, he wasn't looking at me.

"What's up?" I asked, suddenly wary.

He blew out a breath and ran a hand back through his hair. I slowly came to my feet, ignoring Bowie's whine of protest. He looked like a shadow had descended over him. The difference between this morning and right now was night and day.

"Did something happen?"

He cleared his throat and then swallowed hard, as if something was lodged there. "We should...we should talk."

I took a step back. My heart was racing at those words. What the fuck had happened between this morning and my *hour* away at the dorm?

"You're freaking me out. Is everything okay?"

"Yeah. It's just..." He sighed like he hated himself. "You're a freshman in college."

I furrowed my brow. "Yeah?"

"Which makes you...eighteen?"

"Nineteen. Halloween birthday. I told you that last night."

"Right," he said, drawing the word out. "You

mentioned a Halloween birthday, but didn't say how old you'd be on Halloween."

"Twenty," I volunteered.

"Which you didn't tell me because..."

"You didn't ask."

He nodded and glanced away. "I'm twenty-nine, Harley."

"Okay," I said, my stomach starting to knot. "So?"

"So?" he asked, exasperated. "So, I'm ten years older than you."

"I mean, I thought you knew that." I hated the hitch that went into my voice at the words. "I...thought everyone knew I was here for college."

"I knew you were young, but you were drinking."

"College students drink."

"Yes," he said with another huff. "I guess I assumed."

"So, what? What is this, Chase?"

"Look, I'm super into you, Harley. You know that. We have so much in common. Obviously, last night was fucking amazing." He met my gaze firmly but resolutely, and I waited for the other shoe to drop with my heart in my throat. "But we can't let it happen again."

I was going to throw up.

This couldn't be happening. Not after last night. Not after the highest high I had been on this morning. Not after our plans for today.

I shook my head and took a step back, going from sad to furious at the drop of a dime.

"Fine," I spat. "I get it."

"Harley—"

"No, I get it. You got your rocks off, and now, you're over it."

"That is *not* at all what happened," he snarled. "And you know it."

I laughed derisively. "Do I? You're acting just like any other male I've met from the species."

I turned and headed back to the door, but he rushed forward, blocking my way.

"Wait, wait, wait," he said. "That is not why this is happening."

"Then, what is it? You found out I was young, and now, it's over? Because that is the dumbest thing I've ever heard."

"You're not just young, Harley. You're a literal *teenager*. I'm ten years older than you. I run my own law firm. We are in completely different places in our lives."

"I don't care about any of that."

"You will," he said. "You'll care later, and you'll blame me."

I pushed him away. "Don't fucking tell me how I'll feel."

He blew out another breath. "I'm not trying to tell you. And I hate saying that I have the experience of time, but I do. Older guys who go after teenage girls on purpose are not the kind of guys you should want to be with."

"Sure," I said, crossing my arms over my chest. "Loud and clear."

"If you were older..."

I gagged and held a hand up. "Please don't. I just... don't."

He took a step back, fisting his hands into his hair. He looked like he was tearing himself in half. And I wanted to sympathize with him. I wanted to make it all better. But *he* was the one ruining it all. He was doing this. And there didn't seem to be any way for me to fix it.

"Look, Jordan would have killed me before, but his nineteen-year-old little sister? I thought you were twenty-two or twenty-three. Maybe twenty-five if I was being generous."

I paused at that, tilting my head. "Wait, why would my brother have killed you?"

He looked like he was drowning at my question. "Fuck, you don't know who I am, do you?"

"Um...I don't know what answer to give for that."

"Sinclair," he said. "Chase Sinclair."

"Oh...oh," I whispered.

The situation came back to me in bits and pieces. Stops and starts. I hadn't been here when Jordan and Annie got together, but I'd heard the story while out with my family. Annie had thought she would marry someone else until she started dating Jordan, and Jordan had punched the guy in the face when he interfered.

That person had been Chase—*my* Chase. His melancholia at the wedding—the thing that had made me first stop and stare—made perfect sense. He had been watching the girl he'd thought he'd marry walk down the aisle to the man he'd lost her to.

I'd never asked what had become of the guy who could get Jordan Wright to unleash like that. It hadn't seemed important at the time.

I only knew the Sinclair name. The one who had

tried to steal Jordan's girl. Who had broken Julian's heart. Who had tried to sabotage the vineyard. Their enemy.

An enemy I had inherited by virtue of my name.

Oh fuck.

"Yeah. Oh," he said.

"I didn't know you were a Sinclair," I said, suddenly feeling increasingly sicker. "But you knew I was a Wright. You knew that Jordan was my brother. You didn't care about it then!"

"No, I didn't," he admitted.

Then, a horrible thought dawned on me. "Did you do this on purpose to get back at him?"

"What?" he asked. "No."

"No?" I demanded. "Because from where I'm standing, it sure looks like you didn't get what you wanted, so you tried to hurt the person who'd stolen from you."

"That is not what this was, Harley, and you know it. There was no way I could have faked what we had."

I wanted to believe him, but my heart ached from the rejection. I wanted a real reason and not what felt like a made-up difference in our age. "So this has nothing to do with Jordan?"

He sighed again. "I won't lie and say it wasn't tempting at first, but it wasn't what drew me to you. It wasn't why *this* happened. And it has nothing to do with why this can't continue. If I wanted to hurt Jordan, why would I be ending this? I don't care about him. I only care about you."

"Then, why *are* you doing this?" I asked, my heart plummeting with the truth in his words.

"You know why," he said in a whisper, like he hated himself.

Our families despised each other.

Jordan personally hated him.

If I thought my brothers would be mad at our age difference, it was nothing on me being interested in a Sinclair. There would be blood in the water.

In no universe would this work.

I watched the blooming flower I'd held dear in my heart from Chase's attention shrivel and die. My throat was tight with the fight to hold back tears. I wouldn't let him see me cry. I refused to cry.

It didn't matter that I'd met my match.

The first person I'd ever been with who understood me completely.

All that mattered was that it was over.

"Fine," I whispered, choking on the word as I wrenched the door open.

His hand clamped down around my wrist before I could go. "Wait."

"What?" I gasped. "You've made your point."

"I don't want to ask you to—I have no right," he said, the words like broken glass in his throat. "But wait for me."

"You're right," I spat, yanking my wrist free. "You have no right to ask for that."

"I know, and still, I'm asking."

"I won't do it."

He nodded. "I'll be waiting."

"For what?"

"Graduation."

I managed a glare that I didn't feel. Only sick and hopeful and furious and wanting it so badly, all at the same time.

"It's a waste of time."

"Maybe," he said. "I'll be there either way."

I just shook my head and turned and walked out of his house. He might be saying wait, but he didn't mean it. Three years. Anything could happen in three years. In my experience, no one was waiting that long. He'd be long moved on by then. At least this was the reminder I needed that school came first, and I wouldn't forget it again.

PART II

PINING

9

CHASE
AUGUST

"**I**'m not going to this fucking event," I told my father.

"You're going. We need a Sinclair representing the Sinclair Realty interests with the new mayor," my father, Arnold Sinclair, told me.

"Sinclair interests don't interest me. I have my own law firm. That's all that I'm dealing with."

"A law firm that I funded with Sinclair money," he reminded me.

It was the nail in the coffin. He'd given me a huge sum of money to move to Lubbock from Houston, where I'd been working for a successful real estate law firm. My business partner and I had made the move back to my hometown and opened the firm Sinclair & Cruz LLC. But now, my dad held that fact over me all the fucking time.

"Can I just pay you back all the money so that you'll stop using this against me?"

"Could you instead do this small favor that I'm asking of you? What's the worst that could happen? You schmooze with Jensen at a fancy dinner, have a drink, and come home. That's it."

That wasn't it.

That was the *problem*.

Jensen Wright was running for mayor.

He was going to win. That was obvious. But the mayor had not been a Wright in a long fucking time.

And my father always had an in with the mayor. An in that he needed to keep. Which meant we needed a presence with the family that hated us.

The family that I'd avoided like the literal plague since Jordan and Annie's wedding. A point that Ashleigh had made a few times since, but she didn't know the real reason. She thought it was because of Annie. Hell, Annie herself thought I had been avoiding her because of the wedding. They couldn't have all been more wrong.

It was Harley.

I hadn't seen her since the day after the wedding. And as much as it pained me, I couldn't chance seeing her again. I didn't have enough self-control to be in her orbit.

"I won't take no for an answer," my dad said as he strode toward my office door.

I blew out a harsh breath. Great.

"Fine," I muttered. "Just this once."

My dad smiled at me as if he'd already known that he had me under his thumb. And he probably did. I owed him a lot, but how much more would he ask for?

"Thanks, son. This means a lot to me."

I sighed once he was gone and sank back into my office chair. Well, there went my weekend.

Part of me hoped desperately that because Tech hadn't started school yet, she wouldn't even be there. The other part of me was hoping against all hope that she'd be there.

It had been five months since she'd walked out of my door and not looked back. Surely, she'd moved on by now despite how I'd stupidly asked her not to. I'd thought that distance would help me move on, too, but instead, I just missed her.

Tonight was going to be interesting.

I stared up at Wright Construction in dismay.

My office was only a few blocks down Broadway in the historic downtown area, but I almost never drove by here. I hadn't stepped foot inside in since our high school debutante days. They'd rented out the top floor when Ashleigh debuted. The building had been a staple of the community for nearly as long as Lubbock had been incorporated. There was a reason Wrights were royalty here.

"Here goes nothing," I muttered under my breath.

With a deep breath, I straightened my suit and entered the air-conditioned interior. I crossed the white tiled floor to the bank of elevators and stepped inside. It shot straight up to the restaurant that took up the entirety of the penthouse overlooking Tech's campus.

The elevator dinged open on the top floor, and my jaw dropped. I had some vague memory of this place being a subdued business locale that cotillion had turned into a dance floor, but tonight, it was beyond imagination. Fresh flowers blanketed the room. Waiters in suits held trays of finger food and passed out fizzy flutes of champagne. Classical music was a soft melody in the room from the orchestral rendering of a string quartet. It was stunning. Jensen had clearly spared no expense.

"Champagne, sir?" a waiter asked, the brunette smiling up at me as she passed the tray in my direction.

"Thank you."

I took a glass, not missing her fluttered eyelashes, before continuing deeper into the room. It was full of Wrights in every direction. Jensen at the helm of the party with his wife, Emery, at his side. All of his siblings joking around and laughing near the dance floor in formal attire. Jordan and Julian deep in conversation with Weston and Whitton nearby. And then...there she was.

My heart was in my throat at the first glimpse of her in five long months. Her hair was lighter than it had been before and layered into pristine waves. Her lips were an even darker red. So dark that it leaned toward black, but not quite. A quiet nod to her idol, Wednesday Addams. And the dress. My brain short-circuited at the dress. It was a black mesh number that clung to every single curve. The curves that I'd marked with my hands and tongue and imprinted onto my mind. Now, not a single one was hidden under the tight material.

I swallowed and adjusted my trousers. Fuck.

I was going to have to talk to her.

I should absolutely *not* talk to her.

That was a bad idea.

A horrible idea.

The very last idea I should have in the entire world.

And yet...

I was already moving in her direction like a magnet tugged toward its pair. I didn't even notice who she was standing next to until I was nearly there. My eyes slid to the girl at her side, and I barely suppressed a grimace. Eve Houston. The raven-haired vixen who, if rumors were to be believed, had been in a relationship with...my father.

It wasn't the first time he'd cheated on my mother. I knew that. She knew that. But this time, it had been different. This time, it was with someone the same age as his children. He'd gotten her an apartment, lavished her with expensive gifts, taken her on trips. Mom should have left him after that one, but still, she stayed.

When I met Eve's eyes, I could tell that she knew who I was, that we both knew what had gone down. Not that I judged her for what had happened. No, that was all on my father.

"Hello, Eve," I said.

Her eyes widened marginally. As if acknowledging that this interaction was awkward. I probably shouldn't have come over, but I couldn't help it. As my eyes slipped from Eve to Harley, her discomfort skittered out of my mind.

There was only Harley.

The wisps of her blonde hair framing her round face. The little dent in her bottom lip, pronounced in her dark lipstick. Her cheekbones, highlighted with some makeup trick that made them look even higher than before. Her blue eyes were lined with winged charcoal and smoky eye shadow that only made her eyes look brighter than humanly possible. And those eyes were looking right at me.

Not with the anger I had been expecting.

But interest.

A cat looking at a mouse and debating on the right time to pounce.

Well, I was fucked.

"Harley," I forced out, tipping my head in her direction.

That look on her face made me feel like she was gripping me by the throat.

"Chase," she said with that same coquettish smile.

She was completely unbothered by my presence. Just flirting with me, like our weekend had never happened.

Which was what I'd wanted.

Right?

"It's good to see you both," I said.

"You too," Eve said, glancing between me and Harley as if she could see right through us. "Is it just...you representing your family tonight?"

I was glad for the change in subject. Even if it was indicative of the fact that she was nervous about my father's appearance.

"Indeed. Just me."

She relaxed at the words.

"Maybe you can save me a dance later," Harley said.

She arched an eyebrow when my gaze returned to

hers. There was a challenge in her expression. And, oh, how I wanted to meet it.

Instead, I swallowed and said, "Perhaps." I nodded my head at Eve again and then excused myself from the situation.

I could still feel Harley's eyes on me as I walked back across the room, grabbed another glass of champagne, and downed it in one long gulp. Well, that had been...torture.

In the time we'd been together, as short as it had been, I had never once questioned what she was thinking. I'd known from the look in her eyes and the shift of her body and the way she could never keep her perfect mouth shut. I'd known. And now, I had pushed her away and us into uncharted territory.

Fine.

It was fine.

She was over it.

She was over it enough to not give a shit when I spoke to her.

She probably didn't even care that I was here.

And I endeavored not to care either.

"Well, look what the cat dragged in," a voice said as the familiar redhead stepped into my line of vision.

"Annie," I said with a smile.

"Where the hell have you been, Sinclair?" She put her hands on her hips and shot me a pissed look.

"Busy," I offered.

Avoiding the Wrights.

She poked her finger into my chest. "Don't bullshit me. I've known you too long for that. You haven't answered a single text or call. I haven't seen your stupid face around. What's going on?"

I shrugged. "You got married."

"So?"

"Don't particularly think your husband wants us conversing." I tipped my head to the left, where Jordan was currently shooting daggers at me.

"Well, he can fucking deal with it. He doesn't decide who I can and can't talk to."

"The Wrights hate me enough," I said with a laugh. "Must you instigate their abhorrence?"

Annie snorted. "They don't *hate* you."

I raised an eyebrow. "Now, who is bullshitting?"

"They just hate your *family*."

"Perfect."

She laughed and bumped into my shoulder. "Well, I don't hate you or your family. Even if I don't think they've been very kind to the Wrights."

"I haven't done anything to the Wrights."

Lie.

"Uh-huh," she said with an eye roll. "Anyway, it's good to see you. Can we please go get Holly Hop sometime soon and talk like old times? I miss you."

"Sure." Definitely no. "Bring Jordan."

She laughed again, a big guffaw, and covered her mouth. "You're an ass."

"He's seething at me again," I told her.

"Fine, fine. I'll go deal with his emotions. But I'm not avoiding you, you know? This is all your decision."

I rubbed my jaw. "Trying not to get punched again."

She rolled her eyes and knocked me gently on the jaw. "Failing again, Sinclair."

I laughed as she walked back to her husband and immediately watched her making fun of Jordan. His anger at my presence dissipated as she folded into his arms, where she belonged.

At least Annie had done me the service of taking my mind off of Harley. I needed to talk to Jensen, shake his hand, and head out of there. I didn't even want to find my name on one of the calligraphic cards and stay for dinner. I was doing this for my dad. I didn't have to enjoy it.

Jensen was talking to a few gentlemen my father's age when I cut in. He welcomed me with a smile, ever the politician. He thanked me for attending and for the donation my father had already made to the campaign. I wasn't sure how much it was, but it must have been sizable for him to know it had happened.

I decided one more drink, and then I was out of there. It was an open bar after all.

I took my whiskey and Coke out to the balcony and leaned forward against the rail. Only a few people were out there since in mid-August, it was still too hot to exist in West Texas. The temperatures were consistently in the hundreds for days on end, and there was no relief from it in the evenings right now. Usually, the semi-desert climate meant cooler evenings with nice breezes, but nope...not this summer.

"You going to dance with me?" a voice asked behind me.

I took a breath before turning to face Harley. She had

champagne in her hand and looked a little tipsy. "Think I'm going to leave actually."

She took another sip and then moved to stand next to me, close enough that we were nearly touching. "Why did you come to a Wright event anyway?"

"My dad insisted."

"And you do everything daddy dearest says?" she asked.

"No," I told her, my eyes memorizing the lines of her face. "But he paid the start-up for my law firm, and I kind of owe him."

"Ah," she said.

"Plus, he wants an in with Jensen, and"—I shrugged—"hard to say no to a handshake."

She pursed her lips. "So, you're here to schmooze with the mayor."

"I think that's why most people are here."

"Probably. That's kind of gross."

"If only politics were done another way."

She tipped her head back and sighed as if she were suffering. "Why are you *here*?"

"I just told you why I'm here," I snapped. "I know you've clearly moved on, but…"

Her eyes met mine, and I froze, the words dying on my lips. That flirty smile was gone. Whatever mask she'd been holding dropped from her face. And I saw the same desire looking back at me like a mirror.

"I spent all summer in Seattle, interning at a law firm and trying to move on. I even went on a few dates with guys that my old friends had set me up with to see if it would help," she told me. "I hated every minute of it.

Every forced interaction and stupid conversation and fumbled opportunity. And none of it fucking mattered."

"Harley…"

"Take my name out of your mouth," she snarled.

"Okay," I said softly. "Okay. I apologize. You just seemed like you didn't even care that I was here."

"How else am I supposed to act? I wasn't prepared to see you, but there was no other option. It's fucking hard to pretend like I don't want this. Is that what you want to hear?"

"No." I shook my head. "No, I want you to be happy."

She laughed derisively. "You don't want that. You've already wrecked that." She pushed off of the balcony railing. "Go home, Chase."

Then, she turned and walked back inside without a backward glance.

I winced at her retreating back. I'd earned that. And she was right.

I had no right to see her. I had no right to her happiness. I had no right to her.

It was better for me to disappear, just as I had after the wedding.

Still, I watched her until she left my sight, wishing I'd made a different choice. Even though I knew this was the right one.

10

HARLEY

NOVEMBER

I jumped up and down, screaming my head off as they announced Jensen's mayoral win. I grabbed Bailey's hands, and we jumped together. She laughed unabashedly, her freshly dyed dark brown hair swinging around her face.

In the months since Eve's sister had moved in with Whitt and Eve, we'd become close. She was still a senior in high school, but she was the most down-to-earth girl I'd met since moving to Lubbock. Plus, we did all the family interactions together, and she was the closest person to my age in that group.

"He did it!" Bailey called in wonder.

"Hell yeah, he did!" I said. "I need to get us drinks."

Bailey shook her head. "No, no, no. No drinking for me. You know that."

"Sorry. Sorry! I just got excited."

Bailey and alcohol did not mix. Or maybe they mixed too well. She'd gone a little wild before moving to Lubbock but was on the right track now.

"You have a drink though." Bailey pushed me toward the bar on the opposite side of the room. "Don't let me spoil the fun."

"You sure?"

She nodded. "Go. I'm going to hang with my volleyball girls."

"All right," I said, leaving Bailey to the other girls on her high school volleyball team. She was a beast, and I hoped that she'd get to still play wherever she went to college. She'd been on her way to a Division I scholarship until she had to miss her junior year of play.

I passed the rest of my boisterous family. One that I was still admiring I even had. For so long, it had just been me, West, and Whitt. Now, West was in LA with his band Cosmere, and Whitt was busy a lot with Eve. I'd discovered this whole other side of my family—barbecues and lake days and holidays. It was wonderful and overwhelming. I wished that my mom would move down here, but I knew she wouldn't. Not while my grandma and grandpa were still in Seattle.

I ordered a glass of red from the bar and took up a spot to people-watch during Jensen's speech. It was a good one. All about hope and shit. Not about the money and name he'd already had that led him to this position. Alas, politics.

When the speech finished, the crowd roared, and a line formed to shake his hand. And like a magnet, I saw him.

"Fuck," I whispered, melting backward against the wall and taking a formative sip of my wine. "Oh fuck."

Chase Sinclair was at the front of that line.

What the fuck was he doing here?

His father had humiliated Eve at the last mayoral event I attended and made an enemy of Jensen Wright. I couldn't even believe that Chase would be seen at Jensen's victory. I'd thought the rivalry was bad before Arnold blew it up, but now, the Sinclairs were officially public enemy number one.

He was just asking for trouble tonight.

With my eyes still trained on his blond head, I watched two of my cousins, Austin and Landon, approach Chase. Austin clapped a hand on his shoulder, and then they were all talking. Well, arguing. Then, Chase was being bodily turned around and moved toward the door. He pushed off of the guys and ran his hands down his suit before putting his hands up. Landon just crossed his arms and shook his head. The picture was pretty clear. Chase wasn't welcome.

Why had he ever thought he would be?

Was this another plea from his father to make amends?

My curiosity got the better of me, and like a shadow, I slunk through the ballroom, following him as he pushed roughly out a door that led to the elevator bank. His hands were in his hair as he cursed and then reared back and kicked the wall.

"Don't think that's going to do anything," I told him, giving away my position.

He whipped around to find me standing in my black taffeta dress. I hadn't meant to say anything. I was going to leave him to his own devices. After all, the last time I'd seen him, I'd told him to leave. And here he was, doing it before I had to say anything.

Except last time, I'd gotten drunk with worry at his appearance and maybe been a wee bit harsh. And this time, I hadn't even finished my first glass of wine. My heart ached at the sight of him. At his anger and frustration and bruised ego. I shouldn't *want* to alleviate his pain, and yet I could want nothing else.

"Hey," he said, straightening and slipping his hands into his pants. "What are you doing out here?"

"Saw you get kicked out."

"I wasn't kicked out," he grumbled.

"Oh, was it not Austin and Landon pushing you toward the exit? Or did I miss that?"

"Sinclairs are apparently no longer welcome."

"That shouldn't surprise you."

He shrugged. "Did you need something, Harley? Or are you just here to laugh at me with the rest of them?"

I soured at those words. "No, I just didn't know why you'd even risk it after what your dad did."

"I wanted to apologize. To let Jensen know that we weren't all like him."

"Did your dad ask you to do that?"

His lips turned down at the words. "No. There is mutual enmity on that front."

"He brought that on himself."

"Yes. Well, we can't all be as perfect as the Wrights," he said. "And if you're done reminding me of how terrible my family is, I'll do as every Wright here clearly prefers and leave."

I narrowed my eyes. "Don't take your anger out on me."

"I'm not." Then, he blew out a breath. "I didn't mean to. Only that you didn't want to see me the last time we were in a room together. I was planning to *not* see you, and now, you're talking to me. So, what is it, Harley? Should I stay, or should I go?"

"I was just checking on you," I snapped, giving it right back. "Sorry for caring. I'll remember not to do that again."

Then, I turned and pushed the door back open to the ballroom. But I couldn't go back in there and deal with my family. I was hot and frustrated and embarrassed. I should have let him wallow in his pain. Just let him get kicked out by my cousins and been happy about it, like the rest of my family. I shouldn't have let my traitorous heart feel a single thing for him.

So, I turned left as soon as I entered and headed toward the bathrooms. I needed a moment to collect myself before anyone could see me.

"Hey, hey, hey," Chase called behind me.

I whipped around, ready to give him a piece of my mind again, but he just grabbed me by my elbow and tugged me into the little alcove. Our chests nearly pressed together. Our mouths an inch apart. I could smell the sweet scent of his cologne. I could practically taste the whiskey on his lips. My heart stuttered back to life, and I forgot everything that was about to come out of my mouth.

"You cut your hair." His finger twirled a lock of my

short platinum-blonde bob. The dramatic fringe falling nearly into my eyes as I looked up at him.

"For my birthday," I whispered.

"It suits you."

I swallowed. "What are you doing?"

"I have no idea," he admitted. "I never know what I'm going to do around you."

"We're...we're very close," I whispered.

"Should I move?"

"Yes," I said as I shook my head.

He laughed softly as he pushed the lock behind my ear. "I didn't mean to upset you. I was frustrated, and you were right; I took it out on you."

"I know."

"Then you were there, and you told me not to see you again, and..."

"And you should go," I told him.

But still, neither of us moved.

"I should...I should go," I said when he didn't move.

I was going to move.

I had to move.

For my own sanity.

So, I took a step backward. This had gone far enough. Chase was the one who had said we couldn't be together. We were dangerously close to reliving our first experience. In a place *surrounded* by Wrights, who despised him and his family. If *anyone* saw us, I wasn't sure if he'd make it out alive. With my cousin as the new mayor, they could even get away with it.

I took another step. A micro step in my Doc Martens. Then forced myself to do it again.

Away.

Away from Chase Sinclair. And his perfect lips. And stupid dimple. And this dangerous, dangerous desire that sprang up between us like a fount.

I turned, trying to find the courage to flee, and then his hand was on my wrist, yanking me backward.

There were no words.

Just need.

He grasped the back of my head and crashed our lips together. He tasted every bit as incredible as I remembered. Our bodies fit like they were made for this purpose. And oh, I wanted this. I wanted it with every fiber of my being.

But it didn't change anything.

This kiss changed *nothing*.

The age difference still existed. It wasn't going to make my family okay with me dating someone older. Or make our families stop hating each other. This was only going to fan the flames.

And it was unfair.

All of it.

Horribly, wrongfully unfair.

So, despite the fact that I wanted to stay in this moment for all of eternity, I wrenched my head back from him. There was fury in my expression.

"How dare you!" I hissed.

Then, I brought my hand hard against his face. His head snapped to the side, and he stayed here awhile, staring at the wall with fire in his eyes.

My hand stung from the slap, but not as much as the

anger coursing through me. His audacity to think that he'd earned that stolen kiss.

Slowly, he turned his face back to me. The look was of a predator, prowling just under the surface of his skin. The one that said he'd do it again and again and he wouldn't regret it. The one that made me want to let him.

"*You* were the one who said to wait," I snarled. His expression didn't change at my words. "Fuck you."

I couldn't stay another second and deal with this. It was hard enough that I wanted it and had to walk away. It was harder still that I could have it, have *him*, but only in these stolen seconds.

So, I pushed out of his arm and stormed down the hallway toward the back entrance and out of the ballroom. I ignored the elevators and rushed for the ajar stairwell door. I didn't care that I was several stories up. I needed to burn off the energy of that kiss.

Forget that was the last kiss I'd get from him.

At least before, I'd had our perfect weekend to remember.

Now, even that was spoiled.

And I didn't know how to reconcile that with the pain I still felt from his absence.

Wanting him was wrong.

Needing him was worse.

Having him was the hardest of all.

11

CHASE

F uck.

Fucking fuck.

I'd fucked up.

It took me a few seconds to process her leaving. The anger and pain and desire in her expression had mingled all into that one slap. I'd been avoiding another hit from a Wright and not ever considered it would come from Harley. And I'd earned it.

I took off before I could think of anything else to do.

She hadn't deserved it.

I needed to right this wrong.

When I got out to the hallway, she was already gone. Not a sign of her.

"Fuck," I snarled.

I hustled to the elevator bank and slammed my hand down on the button until it finally dinged open a minute later. I pushed for the lobby floor and tapped my foot relentlessly against the metal bottom. It was taking too long. She'd already taken an elevator, and I was going to miss her. And then there was no way to apologize or fix this.

"Fuck," I said again, throwing my fist into the elevator. I shook out my hand, ignoring the pain from connecting with the metal, and bounced from foot to foot, preparing to dash after her.

But as I hurried out of the elevator, the door to the stairwell opened, and a breathless Harley stepped into the lobby.

"No," she said and started walking toward the exit.

"Harley."

"Chase, don't."

She walked through the sliding glass doors and out into the forty-degree weather beyond in her sleeveless dress. She was shivering as she walked away from me.

"Harley, wait, it's cold," I said as I followed at her heels.

"I'm not waiting. I already told you that."

I shucked my jacket off and put it over her shoulders. She jerked to a stop, and I nearly ran into her. She whipped around, her blunt bangs and bob swinging around her face, which was lit with desperation.

"What is this?" she asked as she tugged on the suit jacket. She inhaled sharply, as if even the scent of me on the thing was disarming.

"You were cold."

"That's not what I mean, and you know it."

"I know," I told her. "I know."

"Do you? Are you sure? Because right now, it feels like you're toying with me, Chase." She wrapped the jacket tighter around her. "And it's frankly fucked up. I thought we had something real, and now, you're playing me like a yo-yo. Do you want me? Do you not want me? Is it only fun when you can knock me off-balance? *What is it?*"

"What we had was real. It *is* real," I corrected. I took a step away from her to give her the space she deserved. "And I'm sorry. I fucked up. It's just...I do want you. I do miss you."

"But we can't be together?"

"It's a bad idea," I said, drawing every word out of myself like removing a barbed knife from my stomach.

"Right." Her voice was clipped and disinterested. "Sure. A fine idea to kiss me whenever you feel like it, but not to be more."

I brushed a hand back through my hair and released a puff of frosted air. "You're right. That's fucked up."

"It is."

"I won't do it again."

"You sure?"

I nodded, feeling the life leaving my body at the thought. But I had to be resolute. No more Wright events. No more chances to see her. No more wanting just one more kiss. This was it. This was the end. I'd thought it ended that day when I discovered her age, but this was the real end.

"I'm sure. I'll stay away. I can't imagine why I'd be invited to another Wright event."

"You weren't invited to this one," she reminded me.

"True. Then, I guess it's moot. I'll steer clear. Make it easier for both of us."

Her bottom lip came out into a little pout that made

my heart ache. I wanted to suck it into my mouth and make it all better. But, Christ, she was ten years younger than me. She needed her own life. And if I kept showing up to places where she was, I was only going to drive us both insane.

"Easier," she whispered. "All right. We should shake on it."

I would've laughed if she hadn't looked so shaken up. But still, I held my hand out. For a second, she stared at it and then slowly withdrew her hand from inside the warmth of my wool suit coat.

Our hands brushed together, and she squeezed tight, powerful. The way my old man had trained me to close business deals.

It didn't change the fact that the mere contact sparked between us. An ember to light a bonfire. I wanted nothing more to go back on the deal we'd just struck and pull her into me. This was the end. I needed to stop wanting her. I had to let go.

She slowly removed her fingers from mine. "I guess I should give you your jacket back."

"I'll walk you back inside," I offered. "You can give it to me once you're in the warmth."

"And you?"

"I'll leave," I told her.

She nodded, swallowing. The anger that had rushed through her dissolved into melancholy I understood all too well.

"It's really over," she whispered.

I didn't want to agree. I wanted to hang on to her forever. I'd stupidly asked her to wait for me. To wait until she graduated and she could make an informed decision about what she wanted. It wasn't fair to expect her to know now. And being around each other only muddied the waters.

So, I nodded because the words were stuck to the roof of my mouth like peanut butter.

"And we won't see each other again?"

"That's what's best."

She glanced away, wrapping her arms around her stomach. "Then...then, can I make one more request before I never see you again?"

"What request?" I asked in confusion.

Her eyes found mine again, and in them was a speck of mischief. The girl I'd fallen for so hard and fast that it was like I'd been pushed out of a plane and was plummeting toward the ground without a parachute.

"Just one small thing."

"Anything," I offered her. I'd give her the world if I could.

"Kiss me."

I blinked at her request. That could not have been the words that came out of her mouth.

"Come again?"

"I want you to kiss me."

"Didn't this all start because I *did* kiss you?" I asked.

I wanted to say yes. Fuck, I'd wanted it enough upstairs that I didn't even mind the slap I'd earned when I stole the kiss from her sweet lips. But I had to be wrong here.

"I didn't give you permission for that one. And if I'm never going to get to do it again, I want to remember it the way it was the first time." She took a hesitant step toward me. "Because before, I had that perfect weekend of memories. Your mouth on my thigh in the vineyard, and my body a puddle on your living room floor and your bedroom and…"

My body heated at those words. The memories flooding through me. I remembered them all, too. My mouth on her clit as she had bent over my couch. My cock buried in her pussy as she'd clenched the comforter for dear life. Her face as she had come undone. And every little thing in between—her excitement for the music, her dancing to ABBA, the love for Bowie, the endless conversations, the way she'd looked when she walked in, ready to kayak. Every moment was etched into my mind like a movie reel I could play on repeat.

"Now, my last kiss is the one you stole."

"I see." I took a step between us. "You don't want that to be the one you remember?"

She shook her head. "I want a kiss worth remembering."

I slid my hands inside the jacket I'd wrapped around her shoulders. One moving to her waist. She sucked in a breath as I drew her body firmly against mine. The other up to her jaw, cupping her cheek as if she were the most precious thing in existence.

Her eyes widened. A pant of a breath coming out of her lips. Desire blatant in her blue irises.

My thumb stroked against the dark red lipstick. "I can give you that."

"Can…can you?" she whispered.

She wet her lip, flicking her tongue against my finger.

A challenge more than a request. I smirked down at her. I couldn't resist a challenge.

Then, she tipped her head up and brought my lips down upon her own. Our mouths fit together like they had all those months before. Like the stars had aligned and everything in the entire world made perfect sense. There was nothing but this stretching out for all of eternity.

When I slid my tongue in to meet hers, it was with ravenous intent.

Months had gone by, and my thirst for her had been far from slaked. The desire ran rampant through my chest like a boa constrictor tightening around it. I wanted her. I wanted all of her. One kiss could never be enough.

As the kiss turned from one soft moment to a rush of desperate need, I took the lead, gripping her around the middle and tugging her even harder against me. There was too much clothing in the way. I wanted skin, hot skin against skin. And I wanted it with a fire that could burn the world down.

But that wasn't what I could give her.

I knew better.

I knew better than to let the world burn down with us both in it.

Neither of us would escape getting burned.

And she deserved better than a scorched earth.

So, I let our lips smack one last time, a little drool bridging the tiny gap between us. Her eyes were still closed as I withdrew after giving her the memorable kiss she wanted, but nothing more and nothing less.

"Good-bye, baby girl."

She shivered at the words. Her fingers still fisted in my shirt. Her body limp and pliant.

It took everything in me to wait there and let her eyes flutter open. To see the want there, open and blatant, and know I couldn't give it to her.

So, I walked her to the door, took my jacket back from her, and said good-bye forever.

12

HARLEY

APRIL

"Nice job today," Annie said, bumping me on the shoulder as we walked off the pitch.

"Be real," I said with a laugh.

"What? You're good!"

"I'm mediocre, but thanks."

There was a soccer team that Julian played on called the Tacos. It was a rec league that all of our friends rotated to play on at some point. Since Nora was out of town with West, they'd needed one more girl, and I'd agreed. I wouldn't be leaving for Seattle for another week, and I could fill in since it was the lull before finals. Somehow a serendipitous meetup.

Even if I sort of sucked.

Annie just rolled her eyes at me. "You're too hard on yourself."

"Perfectionists usually are."

"Well, from one perfectionist to another, you were doing great out there. I'm glad that you came and helped out. You could be a regular if you wanted."

I waved her off. "Nah. I can only be so-so at something for so long. And since there's no ice skating here, just going to focus on school."

"Ice skating?" Annie gasped. "You can ice-skate?"

"I'm from Seattle. Absolutely yes. Whitt even played hockey, growing up."

"Whitt! You played hockey?" Annie yelled into the bleachers.

Whitt glanced around as everyone stared at him. "Uh, yes, for a few seasons."

"Hot!"

Jordan just shook his head, striding toward his wife and pressing a firm kiss to her lips. "You're going to be the death of me."

She smacked his ass. "Only if you go down with me. Till death do us part and all that."

"Romantic," he said with a laugh.

"Speaking of till death," Annie said, "I need to check on Chase."

Jordan's eyes clouded over. "Do I even want to know?"

He might not, but I sure did.

"His parents are divorcing."

Jordan remained impassive. "And?"

"And...he's probably a wreck."

"Should I repeat myself?"

Annie smacked him on the chest. "Don't be a dick."

Jordan smirked. "Oh, this is me being reasonable."

"Why are they getting a divorce?" I cut in before they could devolve into a gooey, romantic mess.

Annie turned to me and sighed. "I'm not sure. I'd guess because Arnold is a cheating bastard. Charlotte is *way* too good for him. I can't believe she waited this long to pull the plug."

"That's terrible."

"Tell me about it!" Annie said. "Not that Jor cares, but I'm worried about Chase."

"He's an adult," Jordan said. "He's probably fine."

"Yeah, but he isn't returning my texts or calls. I even texted Ashleigh." She grimaced, checking to make sure Julian was out of earshot. "She, of course, had a million things to say about it, but said she hadn't heard from her brother either. So, he must be really beat up about it. He was always so close to his mom."

"That's awful." I frowned.

I understood that fear. I was that close with my mom, too, and I'd been there through all the worst of the stuff with Owen. I didn't know how I would have survived it all alone. I'd had West and Whitt there for so much of it and my friends from high school.

Doing it all alone would be...tough.

"I just wish he'd let someone in, you know?" Annie said with a shrug. "It used to be me, but now, I'm married to this lug." She punched Jordan again playfully. "And oil and water don't mix."

Jordan shrugged unapologetically. "The Sinclairs dug their own grave."

Julian leaned his way into the conversation. "I heard y'all talking about the Sinclairs. I would like to add my distrust and distaste for them as well."

"We know," Jordan said, shoving him off.

Julian laughed, bumping into Hollin.

"Those fuckers tried to ruin the winery," Hollin said. "Let 'em burn."

Hollin's girlfriend, Piper, shrugged. "Tried to steal my winery out from under me. I second the sentiment."

"Eve," Hollin said, gesturing to Whitt's girlfriend. "Sinclairs, yes or no?"

She wrinkled her nose and gave a thumbs-down.

I swallowed back all the Sinclair hatred. It shouldn't have felt personal. It had nothing to do with me. And yet I felt personally offended for Chase.

"Maybe," Annie said with a sigh. "Still wish I could help."

"I know that feeling," I said.

Annie gave me a thankful look as the rest of our friends and family went on about their Sinclair hatred. Annie and I were in agreement even if she had no idea why I was on her side here.

"Pizza?" Blaire called out to the crowd of players.

"Yes," Annie said as she jogged over to her friend.

I watched her go along with a chorus of people saying yes. It was a tradition to go out to Capital Pizza after the game, but suddenly, my stomach felt all twisted.

Chase's parents were getting a divorce, and he had no one to talk to. He'd cut Annie out. Even his sister couldn't get ahold of him.

He was an adult. As Jordan had reminded us, he could handle this himself, in his own way. But that didn't mean he *should* have to handle it alone.

I hadn't spoken with Chase Sinclair since we'd said our good-bye all those months earlier. I'd had the most memorable kiss of my life. I heard him call me baby girl one more time. My insides melted. And then I'd walked away. Because what else could I have done?

It would be foolish to break the silence I'd personally set up. I was the one who had said he was toying with me by inserting himself into my life. And I couldn't regret forcing this separation.

I'd spent months after looking for him on every corner. It didn't make any sense. Because why would he be on the Tech campus? Why would he come to Wright Vineyard? He had no business at Wright Construction. He'd said he'd steer clear of Wright events entirely. I wasn't going to see him, and it was what I'd asked for.

Still…

I glanced down at my phone, pulling up Chase's phone number in my Contacts. I hadn't had the nerve to completely remove him. I wasn't using the number. What was the harm in keeping it as a *just in case*?

"Harley, you coming?" Whitt asked, his arm slung around Eve's waist.

"I actually really need to work on my history paper," I said.

It wasn't a lie. I did have a history paper due this week. But…it wasn't the whole truth.

"All work and no play makes Harley a dull girl," Eve teased. "Come on. It's just pizza."

"Maybe next time." I waved them off and headed for my Kia.

I sank into the driver's seat, and before I could think better of it, I pressed the button.

The phone rang twice before a voice answered, "Hello?"

"Hey, Chase."

The line was silent a beat too long. "Harley?"

"Hey."

"Hey." He repeated my word back at me. We were both quiet for another few seconds before he said, "Are you okay? Did something happen?"

"Oh, yes," I said quickly. "I'm fine."

"Then...can I ask why you're calling me? I thought... well, it doesn't matter."

"I heard about your parents."

"Oh."

"I'm sorry."

His laugh was sardonic. "I'm not."

"Annie said you're not answering her."

He sighed. "I don't want to talk about it."

"Okay. Can I come over?"

"What?" he asked in a slightly strangled voice. "Do you think that's a good idea?"

No, I really didn't.

"I don't think you should go through this alone."

Another beat of silence.

"Harley, you don't have to..."

"We haven't spoken in months. Do you want to see me or not?"

"Yes," and this time, there was no hesitation.

"I'll be there in fifteen," I told him and then hung up before he could argue.

The map to Chase's house was ingrained in my mind. I hadn't been there in over a year, and it felt like I was going on autopilot to get there. I parked in the driveway and headed to the front door, which opened before I even knocked.

Chase was in board shorts and a blue Yale T-shirt. I, however, was still in my Tacos uniform. I'd only traded out my cleats for black Adidas slides.

His eyes were wide and surprised. "You're in red."

I glanced down at the uniform. "Yeah."

"I've never seen you in anything but black."

"Well, don't get used to it," I said. "This is a special occasion. I was filling in for Nora."

"If you say so," he said with a small smile coming to his lips. "Red looks good on you." He pulled the door open wide, and I crossed the threshold into his house.

I waved him off. "I wear other colors. I crocheted a long off-white vest once. Wore it all the time. It was like festival wear."

"At least white is monochrome. This is like seeing Wednesday Addams in red."

"Pig's blood?" I offered.

He laughed. "Just so."

"And you? Do you always go around announcing that you went to Yale?"

He furrowed his brows. "I don't go around telling anyone I went to Yale." I pointed at his shirt. "Oh. Well, I *was* alone."

"Uh-huh," I teased.

He shrugged. "So what? I went to Yale. At least I'm not lying about it."

I tried not to shiver at the ease that came with his presence. His nonchalance as I made fun of him. The secret smiles that somehow tugged on my heart and reminded me exactly why I'd fallen so hard.

I turned away from him and went to the record shelf. I pulled out a Bowie vinyl and put it in place on the record player. The Bose speaker connected correctly this time and started playing.

"Where is Bowie?" I asked.

"Passed out in his bed." He tilted his head toward the bedroom. "We went on a ten-mile hike and kayaked for a few hours today."

My eyes rounded. "Whoa. I'd be dead, too. How are you standing?"

He rubbed the back of his neck. "Was actually about to go swim. Still have energy to burn off."

"By all means," I said, gesturing to the back door.

He arched an eyebrow. "I don't think you came over here to watch me swim."

"No," I agreed. "But maybe we could sit outside?" My eyes snagged on the couch, where he'd made me completely collapse. "You know...not in here."

His eyes followed my gaze. "Yeah. All right."

We stepped outside and into the warm spring air. Summer was fast approaching, and already, it was heating up. I was just glad dust storm season was mostly on the out.

I sank into a cushioned chair and ducked my feet underneath me while Chase dropped down across from me. For a few minutes, both of us were silent. It wasn't even uncomfortable. I kept glancing at him. My heart and body were trying to remind me exactly how attracted I was to him, and my brain was saying, *Whoa, whoa, whoa! Don't go there again!*

"So, your parents," I finally said.

"Yeah."

"You're not answering Annie about it. Or Ashleigh?"

He kept his gaze on the glittering reflection of the pool. "Just didn't want to make a big deal about it."

"You realize not talking to anyone about it makes it a bigger deal?"

"Guess I see that now," he said with a shrug.

"And you're not unbothered."

He turned to face me, and my cheeks heated at the intensity there. "My dad cheated on my mom enough times that she finally had enough. They were working on their marriage after the last girl, and he promised he wouldn't do it again. But he obviously did it again because he's a narcissist."

"I'm sure he did. Speaking as someone with a narcissistic father, I can say, he'll always do it, and it'll always be someone else's problem. I'm proud of your mom for finally breaking away."

He pushed his hand into his hair. "Yeah. I'm glad she's leaving. I don't know how she's going to survive him."

"She'll have you," I said as if it made all the difference.

His expression changed as if he'd never thought of that.

"My mom had me. I had my brothers. There are

people to lean on, Chase. You don't have to tackle the world alone."

"Sometimes, it feels like it," he admitted.

"Well, you could answer your phone when your sister and best friend call."

"I answered when you called."

My heart rate picked up. I wet my lips and broke the stare. "You did."

"There's another problem."

I glanced back at him. "What's that?"

"I've been working for the company."

I furrowed my brow. "Sinclair Realty?"

"Yes."

"But aren't you working at the law firm?"

He blew out a harsh breath. "Honestly, I'd always had this idea that, eventually, I'd take over the company. But then I got into law, and I was working with Kai."

"Kai?"

"My partner. He moved up here from Houston with me. His wife is from Clovis. So, it was good for them, too. Not completely selfish, but I thought I'd be doing that for another decade before I wanted to start working for the company."

"And that's a problem?"

"Well, I'm working with my dad."

"Ah," I said, seeing the whole picture. "Have you even talked to your mom?"

He flexed his hand. "Yes. She doesn't blame me for working for the company."

"But you feel guilty."

"It feels like I'm choosing him over her."

"That's silly," I said. "Unless you're like me and you have completely no contact with your terrible father, there's no choosing between them. They're both your parents. Your mother knows that."

"What's no contact like?" he asked me, turning his body to face me.

"Excellent. Best decision I ever made. Not that he respects my wishes." I rolled my eyes. "He bought me a BMW when I was home for Christmas."

"Nice gift."

"No!" I argued. "A bribe. I don't want it. I don't want his money."

He nodded. "I get it."

"I'm going home in a week, and he's back in Seattle. I know he's going to try to worm his way back in." I clenched my hands into fists.

"Maybe I should go no contact and see how it feels."

I laughed. "I thought you wanted the company?"

"It's selfish."

"You're allowed to be selfish for things you've worked for, you know?"

He slid off of his chair and sank into the spot next to me. I tensed, expecting...well, I didn't know what to expect. All I wanted was to lean forward and capture another perfect kiss. But that wasn't why I'd come here. I'd been in his place, and I knew what he was going through. And...I'd wanted to see him.

"Thank you," he said simply.

"You're welcome."

"I should probably call my sister."

"Probably. And Annie."

"Jordan is going to hate it."

I winced. "Probably, but she's your best friend. Don't be stupid."

He laughed, reaching forward and tucking a stray strand of my blonde hair behind an ear. I shivered at the touch.

"It was good seeing you."

I cleared my throat and got to my feet. If I didn't get out soon, I was going to break my own heart again. "You needed some sense knocked into you."

"If I ever need it again, I know who to call," he said, thankfully staying seated.

And though I wanted nothing more than to stay, I left.

I left and took my wildly beating heart with it.

13

CHASE

MAY

I pushed myself past the breaking point.

Swam as hard and fast as I could to the small square deck a hundred yards from the shore and then back. I'd made the trek enough times that even Bowie had given up. I'd wiped out my own golden retriever. He was currently sunbathing on the shore with his tongue lolling out from exhaustion.

I was exhausted, too.

I didn't want to take another stroke. But I couldn't stop. Because stopping meant thinking. Stopping meant feeling. Stopping meant I'd have to deal with all the shit that had just been unceremoniously dumped on me.

With a grunt, I pulled myself up onto the deck, panting, my arms like jelly. One more lap. I could do one more. That would be enough.

Then, I heard the sound of car tires on the dirt road that led down to my favorite lake side spot. Bowie jumped to his feet and barked at the Kia that came into view. My stomach flipped at the sight of the little car.

And then the blonde who stepped out of the driver's side.

Bowie went off like a flash, jumping on Harley and nearly knocking her to the ground. He was sopping wet, and even from here, I could see Harley laughing and shaking the water off of her black shorts and tank top.

I dived back into the water and began the trek back toward the shoreline. She put her hand on her forehead when she heard the splash and watched me cut through the water. I was at half the speed that I'd started, but truly, it was a miracle I was still going.

When I stepped out of the lake, waterlogged and drained, she was already moving toward me, a smile on her face.

"Hey, you."

"Hey," I said. I felt like my legs were going to give out as I came up the shoreline.

"How long have you been doing this?"

"Since I called you."

She frowned. "That was, like, an hour ago."

"I know."

Her disapproval deepened. "Maybe you should sit down."

I reached for a towel, drying the water off of my skin before sinking onto the blanket I'd left out for Bowie. Harley dropped down next to me, and Bowie followed, getting up in her face.

She laughed and shook her head. "Still as well behaved as normal."

"I gave up on training," I told her.

"I can see that."

"Thanks for coming."

"I'm glad I was still in town. I leave tomorrow. Though, on the phone, you didn't exactly say what was going on."

A week ago, she'd walked back into my life to help me with my parents' divorce. And I'd certainly thought that was the worst of what was going to happen before she left for Seattle. I hadn't anticipated what had gone down today.

"I know. I'm not sure I wanted to say it out loud," I admitted.

Her eyebrows rose. "That sounds serious."

My eyes traveled down her body. Her feet crossed at the ankles in her signature Docs. Her long, pale legs leading up into the tiny little black jean shorts. Her head tipped back into the sun, and the column of her neck was practically begging me to kiss it.

This was what I wanted. This would help me forget what I'd just heard.

I closed my eyes and looked away from Harley. That wouldn't be fair to her. Not in any world. I might want to roll over and bury my cock in her until we both forgot everything else existed, but that didn't mean it was smart. In fact, it was a terrible fucking idea.

"I can practically hear you thinking," she said.

I laughed. "Well, I'm glad you can't read my mind."

When I met her gaze again, she had an eyebrow raised.

"I don't think it's hard to guess." She tipped her head down toward my board shorts.

Right.

I was soaking wet. And had basically nothing to cover what I was thinking.

"I suppose not," I said and adjusted myself under her scrutiny.

Her cheeks heated, but she didn't look away. "You can't distract me from why you asked me here."

"I could try," I said with that smirk on my lips that I knew was her undoing.

"Okay. You probably could," she conceded. She bit her bottom lip, as if contemplating whether or not she'd let me. "Don't know how much it'd help."

I blew out a harsh breath. "You're right. Remember last weekend, when we talked about my parents' divorce?"

"Of course."

"Well, I thought it was because of my father's cheating."

"It isn't?" she asked skeptically.

"Well it is."

"Say more." She drew her knees up to her chest and wrapped her arm around them as she listened intently.

"I couldn't figure out why my mom finally broke. She'd known about the other girls for literally years. Eve should have been the final straw, and somehow, it still wasn't."

"So, what did he do?"

I sighed heavily. "He got the new girl pregnant."

My jaw dropped. "He didn't!"

"Yep," I said through clenched teeth. "The fucking idiot."

"Wow. I can't believe he was that reckless."

"Neither can I."

"Ashleigh is in her late twenties. He can't want a newborn in the middle of all of this."

I held my hands before me. "I said the same fucking thing. But it's kind of too late, isn't it? The deed has already been done."

"Gross."

"And now, I'm going to have a fucking half-sibling."

"Not the baby's fault."

"Obviously," I ground out. "It's my father's fucking fault. It's always my father's fucking fault."

She sighed and touched my arm. "Do you know who the woman is?"

"No. I'm sure I'll have to meet her at some point. And I don't blame my mom for saying enough is enough. This isn't something she can just ignore, like all the others. This is a very *tangible* reason not to be married to him anymore."

She flopped back on the blanket and covered her eyes. "That is so fucked, Chase."

"Tell me about it."

"No wonder you were swimming until you almost killed yourself."

I ran a hand down my face. "I wish that was all of it."

She flipped open her blue eyes. "There's *more*?"

"The woman works for the company."

"Stop," Harley gasped. "She does not."

"Yep. And the board of directors caught wind of it, and they're *pissed*."

"Well, duh. That's an HR nightmare."

I nodded my head. "They want me to take a bigger

role in the company. Dad would still run everything behind the scenes, but I'd be more the face of the company. They want to keep this out of headlines."

She cringed. "Gross. So, they're going to sweep it under the rug."

I sighed and met her disgusted gaze. "Look, I fucking agree. The whole thing is disgusting."

"This can't be the first time."

"But the first time there's going to be consequences."

"Barely," she snapped. "He knocks up someone who works for him, and the only punishment is, they give his son a bigger position? Man, corporations are all the same, huh?"

"So, you think I shouldn't do it?"

She snorted, coming to her knees and grabbing my hands. "Of course you should take the job!"

I raised my brows. "What?"

"Take the job, silly. Sometimes, the timing isn't right," she said. Her eyes met mine, and I could feel the double meaning behind them. "You just jump anyway."

"Even though I'm stepping in because of my father being a total asshole?"

"Especially so. You want the job. You deserve the job. And frankly, the women of your company deserve someone who will stand up and say that shit stops here."

My eyes met hers, and I knew instantly that she was right. I'd let my intense hatred of my father cloud my judgment. I could do good here. I could be different from my father. I could maybe even save the Sinclair name.

"You're right," I said.

"Of course I am."

"I'll take the job."

"Duh," she said with a laugh as she pulled me to my feet and threw her arms around me. "You'll do great."

She was perfection in my arms. All I wanted was to put aside the divide we'd agreed upon. I wanted to live here in this moment. But I knew that wasn't possible.

I couldn't take over my father's company in the wake of a potential scandal with a twenty-year-old at my side.

I'd look just like him to the board.

Just like my father in every way.

Even though I was nothing fucking like him.

And the worst of it was that I could never let her know that my thoughts went there. That I wanted her to be at my side through all of it. We'd drawn the line in the sand. It was better that we kept it exactly where it was.

14

CHASE
OCTOBER

"Did you hear me, Chase?" Ashleigh asked.

I glanced up at my sister over the edge of my computer screen. I'd zoned out again with her diatribe. I'd taken a bigger role in the company, stepped right into my father's shoes, and gained my sister as an unwanted accomplice.

"Ash, I really don't want to deal with this right now."

She rolled her eyes. "These are important topics. We need to be on board."

"Just handle it," I snarled.

Ashleigh jerked to her feet. "I never thought you'd be worse than Dad."

"Go talk to him then." I gestured down the hall.

"He's busy," she whined.

I pinched the bridge of my nose. "It's been a long day. It's Halloween. We shouldn't even still be here. Don't you have a party to attend or something?"

"Obviously. We're both supposed to be at that charity ball in two hours. Tell me you didn't forget."

I'd forgotten.

"Of course not."

She rolled her eyes. "I'm sending you the invite again. What are you dressing as? You have to be in costume."

"I was just going to wear a suit."

She sighed heavily through her nose. "I did not sign up for being your personal assistant. I'll have something sent to your house as well."

"You're not my assistant."

"Whatever," she said dismissively. She snapped her iPad case over the screen. "It's already done."

I waved her off as my phone dinged. A smile spread on my lips when I saw the text from Harley, which included a picture of her pointing at a plethora of alcohol.

Think I can go twenty one for twenty one tonight?

"God, who is she?" Ashleigh asked.

My head snapped up. "Who is who?"

"The girl you're always messaging. I'm not stupid. I can tell you're seeing someone."

"I'm not seeing someone."

Ashleigh leaned her hot-pink-clad hip against my desk. "Brother of mine, do I look like an idiot?"

"Do you want an honest answer?"

She huffed. "You're always secretly smiling at your phone."

"I am not."

"Fine," she said, holding her hands up. "I give up. Have your secret girlfriend. I don't need to know."

I rolled my eyes. "You have needed to know every detail of everyone's lives since you were born."

"Then, tell me!" she gasped. "Is it my friend Bee?"

I blinked at her. "Good-bye, Ashleigh. I'll see you at the party later."

She sighed heavily. "You're no fun."

I waited for her to leave before responding to Harley's message.

Try not to die of alcohol poisoning.

Don't spoil my fun, Sinclair.

Birthdays aren't as much fun at the hospital.

It's my 21st. I'm allowed to go OTT.

I shook my head at the picture she'd sent of her with a bottle of tequila tipped to her mouth with the words *got salt?* under it.

She was going to be the death of me.

All those months earlier, Harley was the only person I'd let near me about my parents' divorce. Things had changed with us. I knew how I felt, but also that we couldn't be together, not when things were so precarious in my new position. But I couldn't stay away again.

So, we'd begun texting. She'd been in Seattle all summer, and in some ways, it was easier to message her, knowing she was thousands of miles away and I couldn't rush straight to her. She'd come back at the end of August for school, and I'd managed to maintain distance.

Though our texts were becoming more and more frequent.

Make sure you have a DD.

What do you think you are?

I laughed. Yeah, sure. I could imagine me showing up at a college party for her twenty-first birthday. This was what I'd meant from the beginning. Our lives were too different.

She was going to go twenty-one shots for her twenty-first, and I was being dragged to some fancy charity Halloween party. I was certain we couldn't be further apart than tonight.

Still, I couldn't keep myself from replying.

If you need me, Wright, I'll be there.

I waited for her response, but it didn't come. I sighed and shoved my phone into my pocket. I'd deal with that later. After this stupid party.

There were Wrights at the party.

Ashleigh had not warned me that there would be Wrights at the party.

I crossed my arms over my chest in the brown leather jacket that my sister had sent over, along with a brown Stetson fedora to complete my Indiana Jones costume.

Luckily, it wasn't Jordan and Julian, but I'd had enough run-ins with the other side of the family that I wasn't particularly happy to see any of them either.

"Chase," Ashleigh said with a smile as she approached me in her Barbie holiday ball gown. Her elbow-length-gloved arm was linked with a girl in a skintight black leather cat costume.

"You didn't tell me Wrights would be here."

Ashleigh widened her eyes and tilted her head at the cat. "Chase, this is my friend Layla."

"Hi," she said, fluttering her eyelashes at me. "I've heard so much about you."

"Nice to meet you," I said, trying to care and coming up lacking.

Ashleigh had been trying to push all of her friends on me since I'd taken over the company. Apparently, I was a charity case now.

Then, I returned my attention to my sister. "You didn't mention Wrights."

"Jesus, Chase, they own the town. Just assume they'll be here."

"Do you want to get a drink?" Layla asked.

"Layla is a speech language pathologist professor, Chase," Ashleigh said, nudging me.

"That's nice. I'm not drinking tonight."

"What?" Ashleigh asked in confusion. "Whyever not?"

"I want to be able to drive home." I nodded my head at Layla. "If you'll excuse me."

Then, I walked across the room to avoid my sister and her latest hope for me. Layla might be a delight. A speech language pathologist sounded lovely. But if it was a setup from my sister, I wasn't interested.

I wandered the room, shaking hands with business partners and steering clear of Wrights. I made eye contact with Morgan Wright, the current CEO of Wright Construction, long enough to know that I wasn't wanted and moved on. The night was getting late by the time the rest of the attendees were beginning to appear intoxicated. Enough so that I was second-guessing whether or not I should have had a drink this whole time.

Or just gone home.

I should do another circuit of the room, schmooze with the other business owners and all of that good networking bullshit.

But it was Harley's birthday.

And I hadn't heard from her in hours.

I was sure she was having a good time, drinking herself sick. That was what college students were supposed to do. And they didn't need someone ten years older worrying about them.

"Fuck," I grumbled. "I should just go home."

I left and headed to my car when my phone went off. I checked the message and saw a picture of Harley holding up a shot of some clear liquid.

take a bday shot w me

What number are you on?

lost count

sharpie marks on arm are blurry

Sharpie marks? Were they marking the number of drinks on her body?

or maybe seeing double ???

Great.

Do you need me to pick you up?

that's not what I need from u

What do you need from me?

come find out

The text was followed by a picture of her cherry-red lips making a kissy face. Then a follow-up of the bar name where she was currently located. A bar that was a mere two minutes from my current location.

Fuck it.

Harley stood on the side of Broadway when I miraculously found a parking spot for my Porsche outside of the bar. I'd nabbed it right as someone was leaving. I stepped out and froze at the sight of her.

She'd conveniently not shown me a full picture of her

costume for the night. And I should have fucking guessed.

"Harley Quinn," I said with a smirk.

She did a twirl straight out of the movie, and my cock lurched. Her blonde hair was up in pigtails. The ends dyed blue and red. She had on the quintessential ripped tee that said *Daddy's Lil Monster*, tiny blue-and-red shorts, fishnet tights, and heeled boots.

"You made it." She stumbled off the curb and strode in my direction. She tumbled slightly, leaning against the hood of my car. A laugh left her lips, as maniacal as her namesake. Then, she sprawled onto my car. Her back arched, and she pushed her hands up over her head.

I stepped up to her and raised an eyebrow. "You're drunk."

"Legally," she said with a giggle.

"Better than our first meeting."

"Nothing is better than that," she said, closing her eyes and sighing. "Is it supposed to be so...spinny?"

"Common side effect, yes." I pushed my hands into the pockets of my jacket to keep from reaching for her. "Where are your friends?"

"Left 'em inside."

"No one cared?"

She shrugged. "Wanted to see you." She slid off of my car with mischievous intent in her eyes. "Wasn't sure you'd come."

"Well, I'm here now."

"You are, aren't you?" she said, tilting her head to the side. She reached forward and ran a hand down the front of my leather jacket. Her lips tilted dangerously upward. "Do you have the whip too?"

"Harley..."

Her hand moved to the buttons of my shirt, trailing her fingers up the line of my chest. "You know it's my birthday."

"I do, in fact. I came to make sure you got home safely."

She took another step in. Our chests nearly touching as her hands tangled in my collar. "Do you know what I want for my birthday?"

I remained perfectly still. "I think I can guess."

"I can tell you in explicit detail," she purred.

"You're drunk," I repeated.

"Doesn't change anything."

I gripped her wrist in my hand. "Unfortunately, it changes everything."

She stuck out her bottom lip. "You don't want me?"

"That has never been our problem."

"So, you do want me?"

"I want to see you safely home."

"To your home?" she asked, leaning all of her weight against me.

My cock stirred at her closeness. If I were a different person, a different guy...

But I was not that guy. I'd made the choice about us at our first meeting. We could fuck. Man, could we ever fuck. I'd have her bent over my bed all night for how much I wanted her. That hot, feisty mouth and her tight little body and wet fucking pussy. Every fiber of my being wanted that with her.

Oh, how I hated being the bigger person.

"To your house."

She shook her head. "Nope. Your place."

"Get in the car, Wright."

Her eyes lit up. Wasted drunk and still defiant as hell. "I want to be in your bed."

I exhaled and then finally nodded. "Fine. Stay in my bed."

That didn't mean anything was going to happen. But I didn't feel comfortable leaving her here. Not when her friends had let her wander off, we were this close to bar close, and as far as I knew, she didn't have another way home.

So, I helped her into the passenger side and drove home.

It had nothing to do with wanting her there.

Nothing at all.

15

———

HARLEY

"Chase?"

He kept his eyes on the road as he pulled into his neighborhood. "Hmm?"

My head was spinning a million miles a minute. I couldn't believe he was here. I couldn't believe we were going to his house. I couldn't believe any of it.

I leaned across the seat. His hand was on the stick shift, and I threaded my fingers through his on top of it. He breathed out heavily, but didn't move it.

"Can we call a truce?"

"A truce?" he asked.

"Mmhmm."

"What is involved in this truce?"

"You fuck me."

He choked on a laugh. "Harley, you're drunk."

"I'm not *that* drunk."

His eyes shot to mine in disbelief. "Uh-huh."

Okay. I was *that* drunk. I had a line of black Sharpie marks up my arm that listed all the drinks I'd had. Way too many. I'd almost thrown up halfway through the night, and my head was still spinning.

But God, I wanted his cock inside of me. I wanted it so fucking bad. Like I'd never wanted it before.

He parked the Porsche in the garage and came around to the passenger side as I tried to step out. Instead, I nearly ate it, barely catching myself on the door to his Subaru.

"Fuck," I bit out.

"Come here. I got you."

I tried to step toward him and tumbled forward again. He caught me in his arms before I could fall. I started giggling. Suddenly, it was all hilarious.

He shook his head, kicked the door closed, and lifted me effortlessly into his arms.

"Oh!" I gasped.

I was a rag doll, limp, my head lolling back. The whole world felt upside down.

"I've never had this much to drink in my life."

"I can believe that," he said as he carried me across the threshold.

"It's so freeing to not care."

He pursed his lips. "How so?"

"I always care so fucking much." My hands knotted in the leather jacket. "I have to be perfect. In school, I have to maintain a 4.0. I need to keep my scholarship. I have to get into the best law school."

"I understand that life. I went through that."

"Yeah. Yale. Where did you go to law school?"

"UT Austin."

"That's a good school."

"My dad was disappointed," he said flatly.

"Fuck him."

Chase laughed. "Yes, well, I mean to say that you can only make the decision for yourself."

"I don't even know if I want to be a lawyer."

The words hit me in the gut. The words I'd never uttered to anyone. Certainly not to my mom, who had slaved to get me the best education so I could pursue my dream. Or my brothers, who always believed I would change the world. Definitely not to my dad, who I never told anything.

It was hard enough, admitting it to myself. Let alone to someone else.

"You don't have to decide today," he said wisely.

I just laughed. "No one makes you think you have time to wait."

"No one else matters right now."

"Just you?"

"Just you," he corrected. "Can you stand?"

"Maybe."

He tried to put me down on my feet in the living room, and my legs gave out.

He chuckled and set me down on the infamous leather couch. "What are we going to do with you?"

"I can think of a few things."

He ignored me and then began to slowly unlace the heeled boots that brought the entire outfit together. He pulled one shoe off and then the other.

"That seems a little safer," he said.

I came to my feet again, turned toward the bedroom, promptly tripped on the couch, and fell face-first into it.

My ass was hanging high in the air. I was wearing basically nothing but a scrap of red-and-blue fabric.

"Oops," I said.

Chase slipped his hands around my waist, pulled me back to my feet, and then lifted me over his shoulder. "You're a mess, Wright."

"My head is spinning."

"We'll get you taken care of."

"Is it bad that I might not want to be a lawyer?"

"It's fine. Law degrees are overrated."

"You have a law degree," I pointed out.

"That I'm not currently using. So, it doesn't matter. You don't need one unless you want to practice law. You can accomplish all your dreams without it. I promise it's not something you go into lightly. It's the worst three years of your life. So, you need to know."

"Oh."

"But you don't need to know now. You have time."

As soon as Chase opened the door to his bedroom, Bowie raced around our feet. Chase smiled and tried to brush his dog off, but Bowie was unperturbed. I giggled, reaching for him over Chase's shoulder.

He grunted as I nearly toppled backward out of his arms, and he tossed me onto his enormous bed. Bowie bounded onto it, licking my face.

"Good boy!"

Chase shook his head. "Off the bed, Bow. Come on. Let's go out."

Chase was gone for a minute, and I collapsed backward. Why was I having a serious conversation about law school when I was drunk and just wanted dick? I really needed to let that go and focus on what mattered *right now*.

Like lying in Chase Sinclair's bed.

When Chase returned, he'd ditched the jacket and fedora.

"No Indy for me?" I asked on a pout.

He raised an eyebrow. "You're into Indiana Jones?"

"What woman isn't?"

"I'll keep that in mind." He strode to the bed and looked down at me with conflict in his eyes. "Now, what are we going to do with you?"

"You could just do *me*," I said, turning his words around. I sat up, reaching for his belt and tugging him closer.

"You make this very difficult," he said as if he were truly suffering.

I smirked. "Good."

"Now, who is toying with whom?"

"It's my birthday," I said, sliding the belt out of the loop.

"I realize it is your birthday."

"And I'm here."

"Yes," he said.

I popped the button on his pants. "And I want you."

He clenched his jaw. "But..."

I dragged the zipper down. "You want me."

"That's not the point."

"It feels like the point," I said as I tugged his shirt out from the waist of his pants. "It feels like the whole point actually."

"You're going to regret this in the morning."

But my mouth was on his heated skin, a kiss to the V that led down to what I really wanted. He groaned, and I pressed my palm against his cock. He was already getting hard for me.

"I don't believe in regrets," I said.

"Harley..."

I looked up at him, my hand on his lengthening cock. "Fuck me. Fuck me like you mean it."

His head dropped back. I swore I saw torture cross his face. As if he was in physical pain at my words.

"I..." He growled in the back of his throat. "I didn't bring you here for that." Then, he stepped back, away from me, and refastened his pants.

"I deserve a present."

"I got you a present."

I blinked up at him. "What?"

"I wasn't sure I'd see you to give it to you," he said. "But I thought, on the off chance I did..." Then, he removed a small blue box from his pocket.

Even I wasn't drunk enough not to recognize Tiffany's.

"What is it?" I whispered.

"Open it and find out."

My fingers slipped on the white ribbon as I pulled it loose and then popped the top. Inside was the letter *H* on a circular silver pendant attached to a long chain.

I must have stared at it, speechless, a bit too long because he said, "You don't like it."

He reached for it, and I yanked it back, holding it to my chest.

"No, I love it. It's mine."

"Good," he said with relief in his voice.

"Put it on me?"

I turned on the bed as best I could, moving the ridiculous pigtails out of the way. He slid the necklace into place and clasped it from behind. It settled like it had always belonged there.

I stroked the *H* and then looked back at him over my shoulder. "You're going to give this to a girl and not get in bed?"

"I'll get in bed," he finally conceded. "But just to sleep."

"Okay," I relented.

"Let me get you something to sleep in." He walked into his closet and came out with an oversize T-shirt and shorts. "Here."

I took the clothes out of his hands and arched an eyebrow. "Are you going to watch?"

"Oh, uh...I'll just..."

Then, he returned to the closet.

I giggled and tugged on the T-shirt. It came down to my knees, so I opted out of the shorts and crawled into bed. As soon as my head hit the pillow, the entire night came back to me in a head-pulsing mess.

Oh no.

Oh no, no, no...

"You ready?" Chase asked, stepping back into the room, shirtless.

"Um..."

Then, I hurried past him and hurled the entire contents of my stomach into his toilet. I groaned as I continued to bring up more and more alcohol. When I thought I was finally done, I flushed and staggered away from the toilet. Chase had a spare toothbrush waiting for me next to a bottle of Gatorade and two Tylenol.

"My hero," I whispered.

I downed the Tylenol and brushed my teeth. Then, I found a washcloth and removed as much of my makeup as I could manage. After, I carried the Gatorade to bed, hugging it to my chest like a life raft. "I feel awful."

"Based on the marks on your arm, I'd assumed you would."

He took the Gatorade from me, set it down, and pulled back the covers. I sank onto the bed with a groan. Then, with a gentleness I barely knew how to process, he removed the hair ties from my hair, letting my locks fall to my shoulders, tucked my legs up into the bed, and pulled the covers over me.

"You're being so nice."

His expression softened. "Believe it or not, I care about you."

"Yeah, but…"

"No but," he said. "Just get some rest."

"Wait," I said as he crossed the room. "Where are you going?"

He grinned. "To get the lights. I'm coming back."

I relaxed back at that pronouncement. He flipped the lights off and got into the bed. His hand rubbed my back, soothing me toward unconsciousness. I felt blackout approaching.

"Chase," I murmured.

"Hmm?"

"Graduation, right?"

He was silent, his hand stilling on my back. "I don't expect you to wait, Harley. I want you to live your life."

"I'm studying abroad in London next semester."

"Good," he said without hesitation.

"But you'll wait?" I whispered.

He was silent for long enough that I thought he might have fallen asleep.

"I'll wait," he confirmed.

And then I fell into oblivion.

16

HARLEY
JUNE

"Mom, it's not a date," I insisted.

"You're wearing eyeliner. You blew out your hair. You're in a dress," Mom pointed out, leaning against the doorframe to my childhood bedroom.

"And?"

"And you don't do those things for just anyone. You've been back from London for three weeks, and I haven't seen you in anything but lounge clothes or a suit for that law office."

I shrugged. "It's just a friend."

"A friend who is a boy."

"Yes."

"Who is coming all the way to Seattle to see you."

"Well, no. He's visiting friends in town."

"You're his friend, and he's visiting you."

I rolled my eyes. "It isn't a date. I'm going to show him around downtown. We're getting lunch. It's no big deal."

"Do I get to meet Mr. No Big Deal?"

I stalled at that thought. What would my mom think

if she saw Chase Sinclair? No one knew we were even friends. Let alone anything else that had happened. Mom probably wouldn't be happy that he was so much older than me. But I hadn't been lying when I said it wasn't a date. He wasn't in Seattle for me. But...I didn't mind seeing him.

It had been a long semester abroad with the time difference. I'd had my fun, like he'd insisted I should have. I'd lived my life. But still...my heart remembered that graduation was only around the corner.

"If he's just a friend, then I can meet him."

"Fine," I said on a laugh. I put on the *H* necklace Chase had given me for my birthday, clasping it behind my neck and letting the pendant dangle low. "If you want to meet him, Mom." I pressed a kiss to her cheek. "I love you."

"I love you, too. Have fun, sweetheart."

My phone dinged, and I saw the text from Chase, saying he was outside. "Okay. He's here. I'll see you later, Mom."

My mom shot me a look of amusement, but I ignored it and headed outside. Chase was idling in a blue Porsche that matched the red one he had at home. Only he would spend the money on a rental this fancy.

"Nice car," I said, slipping into the passenger seat.

"You know I like my cars."

"I do."

He smiled down at me. "Good to see you."

I swallowed. "It is."

I eyed him, my heart in my throat. Eight months since I'd seen him, five thousand miles apart, and a six-hour time difference, and it was like no time had passed at all. He was in dark denim, a white button-up, and boots. Ray-Bans covered his baby-blue eyes. His blond hair was short and brushed to the side, but he had a five-o'clock shadow that I'd never seen on him before. My hand came out and brushed across the stubble.

"Growing a beard?" I asked.

He inhaled sharply and rubbed his jaw. "Nah, just a late flight last night, and I didn't feel like shaving this morning. Should I get rid of it?"

I shook my head. "No, it looks good on you."

He smirked. "Noted." His hand came out to brush against the *H* necklace he'd given me. "You still wear it?"

I flushed slightly. "Yeah. It's my favorite."

His face was unreadable for a second before a pleased smile slowly crossed his lips. "Good. Now, where are we headed?"

And that *good* made my entire body turn to goo.

I gave him directions to downtown, and soon, we were pulling into a parking garage near Pike Place Market. It wasn't my usual haunt, but it was classic Seattle. If friends were visiting, this was where you brought them.

We strode through the quintessential sign with Public Market Center in bright red letters before stepping into the open-air market. We walked past the markets with fish that had come fresh off the boats that morning, a variety of butcher-paper-clad flower vendors, as well as fresh produce, shops, and restaurants. Finally, we stopped at my favorite mom-and-pop shop and ordered lunch. When our food came out, we took it to an outdoor patio with big red umbrellas to block the afternoon sun. The fish was as incredible as ever. It was one of the big things I missed about the city when I was in Lubbock.

I cajoled Chase into ice cream cones. I got strawberry, and he got chocolate. For once, the sun was shining without a cloud in the sky. It probably wouldn't last long. It never did. But right now, it was a perfect day.

"So, the friends you're visiting," I said as we strolled the pier, "when are you meeting them?"

"Tonight for dinner. We have a reservation for seven."

"That sounds fun."

"Yeah. They had to take their son to a baseball tournament for most of the day."

"So, you can spend the day with me."

His eyes tracked me as I took a long lick of my ice cream. The heat melting the soft cream faster than I could lick up.

He cleared his throat. "Uh, yes. Lucky that way." He ran his tongue along the cone to keep it from melting in a similar fashion to mine.

I swallowed, remembering precisely what that tongue could do to my body. I didn't entirely remember everything that had happened the night of my birthday. But I remembered throwing myself at him like I'd die without his dick. I'd woken the next morning, mortified by my behavior.

But it didn't mean it had been a lie.

I was the living definition of *distance makes the heart grow fonder*.

I leaned against the railing that looked out over the

harbor beyond. Ice cream was melting toward my hand, and I lapped it up. Our eyes met again, and I could tell that he was thinking the same fucking thing as me.

I needed to change the subject.

"How do you know these friends?"

"Yale," he said quickly. "Curt was my roommate freshman year. He's a marine biologist now."

"That's a fun job. Why didn't we decide to go into a fun career?"

He laughed. "No one ever said law was fun—that's for sure."

"But most people aren't basically running a company at thirty either," I pointed out.

"Touché." He tipped his ice cream cone to me in salute. A trail of chocolate ran down his thumb. He cursed under his breath and brought the digit to his mouth.

My mouth went dry as he licked the offending cream off of his finger. I crossed one leg over the other in hopes of stopping the pulsing in my core. Fuck.

"Are you still set on law?" he asked.

I jerked my head back to my own ice cream. "I mean, I took the LSAT in February, and I'm studying all summer to take it in July."

He arched an eyebrow at me. "That's not the same thing as being set on going."

I shrugged. "I don't know. It feels like what I should be doing. It's what I've been working toward."

"Again, not the same thing."

"I'm at a disadvantage with you since I got wasted and told you all about my fears."

He leaned toward me and tipped my chin up to look at him. I felt frozen in his embrace.

"I feel like that is an advantage. There's no pretense between us. So you can tell me exactly what you think. I've seen you throw up in my bathroom. I think I can handle the rest."

I laughed. "Thanks for reminding me."

"I'm just saying that changing your mind at twenty-one is perfectly normal. And if you don't want to be a lawyer, Harley, then you shouldn't go to law school."

If I didn't want to be a lawyer...then I shouldn't go to law school.

It was that simple.

And somehow forever difficult.

"But I still feel like law is the best way for me to be able to make a difference," I told him, pushing off of the railing and continuing forward.

"How so?"

"Well, I want to...help women and minorities and LGBTQ with workplace problems. I want equality and inclusion and resources that aren't there yet. I want to be part of the solution for a problem that feels as if it is growing ever more divisive."

"That's ambitious."

I shot him a grin. "Have you met me?"

"Well, I believe you can do it."

"Yeah?"

"Changing the world starts with one person."

My smile was radiant then. "Thanks. Yeah."

"Though I think you can do it with or without a law degree. You just have to decide if that's what you want."

I nodded. "Yeah. I guess."

"Enough work talk," he said. "I haven't seen you since you left. What have you been doing since you got back?"

I finished off my cone, wiping my hands clean and tossing the napkins into a nearby trash can. My arms swung at my sides as we walked together. Then, halfway through my story about how I'd started to take up ice skating lessons again, his hand moved into mine.

My head whipped up in surprise at the contact. Then, he threaded our fingers together. Just a couple walking through the market on a sunny day, hand in hand. My entire body felt like it was on fire. What was happening? He was holding my hand? Was this actually a date?

Yes, he was here to see his old Yale roommate. But he was here to see me, too, right?

I could just enjoy this. And not overcomplicate things.

It was the first time we'd ever been in a place where neither of our families was around. No Wrights to catch us together. No Sinclairs in sight. No one to question why we were here like this. No one who knew that our families hated each other. No complications at all.

Except the ones that we'd never been able to avoid.

Because what would happen when we went home?

It didn't change everything when we returned. And somehow, I couldn't care. I could only remember the way he'd licked ice cream off of his thumb, desire in his eyes while they were on mine.

But we were out of time. He had to take me home. He was here to see his friend. I didn't know what I was going to do if I didn't take this opportunity.

We were in the parking garage before I plucked up the courage to ask, "What is this?"

He stopped. "What do you mean?"

"You're holding my hand."

"Should I not?"

I shook my head. "I just...what are we doing? I threw myself at you at Halloween, and you turned me down. You don't even want me. I just..."

But whatever had come out of my mouth was *wrong*. So wrong.

I watched his eyes flash with fury at the suggestion. Then, he was backing me up. I took a step back and then another, my heart hammering in my chest.

"Are you fucking kidding me?" he snarled. "The fuck I don't."

My back was against the wall of the garage. The darkness enveloping around us, tucking us safely away from any onlookers.

"Oh," I whispered.

"I think you must not remember what happened on Halloween," he said, his hands sliding over my hips to my waist and then up my sides. "I could barely fucking contain myself around you. I only stopped because you were not sober enough to consent."

"I...I...yes."

His hands pushed up into my hair. My body went limp as he took command of me. "I've wanted you so fucking bad every single fucking day since."

"Please," I begged.

There was no restraint left. No room for thought. Just

his lips crushing against mine. His tongue in my mouth. His hands pushing my dress up to my hips.

I fumbled with his belt, ripping it open to get to him. Then, his cock was in my hand. He groaned into my mouth. All the buildup from restraining ourselves all this time came forcefully to a head.

"Need to be inside of you," he said.

"God, yes."

Then, he lifted me by my thighs. I wrapped my legs around his waist and held on to his shoulders. He angled our bodies together and then thrust home.

My head fell backward against the hard concrete as a cry escaped my lips. Fucking hell. This was what I'd been missing. What I'd wanted for so fucking long. It didn't matter how much time had passed since I'd been with him; I'd never forget the wild weekend we'd shared two years ago.

Though I'd wanted nothing more than this, I'd honestly never thought it would happen again. We'd been talking on and off for a year. I couldn't have gotten any more blatant than I had on my birthday. But my brain must have scrambled it all up. I'd sworn he was over it. That it had just been...him being nice. That I was the one still pining.

I'd gotten flirty from him in London when we had the time difference lined up to chat. But it wasn't until I saw the fire in his eyes that I knew.

He'd been holding himself back.

He wanted me just as fucking bad as I wanted him.

His mouth covered mine as I came on his cock. He barely made it a handful of more thrusts before finishing inside of me. Our chests heaved. His forehead fell against mine.

And as we came down from the incredible high, I knew that I was ruined.

I'd wait.

I'd keep waiting.

I'd wait forever.

17

CHASE

Well...

Fuck.

I hadn't intended to fuck her.

I told myself I wouldn't.

Then, we were strolling along. I had her hand in mine. The entire world felt peaceful and perfect and just...right. Like we should have been doing this all along. Even though I knew we couldn't.

That we shouldn't be doing any of it at all.

But I was a sucker.

And I was lost to her.

I'd missed the fuck out of her when she was in London. I'd told her to go. I'd told her to live her life there, and I assumed she had. I was sure that she'd met some London boy. I was jealous of every moment.

A feeling that I knew was wrong to feel.

When I'd found out she was returning to Seattle and not Lubbock, I'd decided, without a second thought, that I had to see her. Sure, I was visiting Curt. I hadn't seen him in ages. His wife and kids were incredible, but I'd be lying if I said it wasn't for her.

Now, my cock was inside of her, and she was panting breathlessly under my body, and I couldn't regret it.

Wouldn't regret it.

But I didn't know what the fuck I was going to do now.

"Harley…"

She pushed her lips against mine again, breathing the words, "Let's just enjoy it."

So, I gave up.

I would enjoy it. For as long as I could.

I withdrew from her body. We both righted our clothing. Neither of us able to contain the smiles on our faces. I wanted nothing more than to take her to my hotel and spend the rest of the weekend buried between her legs.

Unfortunately, I'd made plans with Curt because I was sure I could resist her. I'd been wrong. So very wrong.

So I had to drive her home.

"You could come to dinner," I blurted out once we were in the car.

Her eyes widened. "With your friend?"

"Yeah. His wife is coming."

"Oh shit, I was going to have movie night with Mom." She bit her bottom lip and then said slowly, "I could cancel?"

"Don't cancel on your mom," I said automatically.

"I didn't think we'd…that this was…" She trailed off.

"Same," I agreed without her having to finish.

She sighed. "But I kind of want to cancel now. You're

only here for another day, and I won't be back in Lubbock until August."

"I know."

"Let me text her," she decided.

I should have pushed back. This wasn't the bargain we'd made. But she was right. I wouldn't see her again until August. Maybe I was being selfish, but fuck, I wanted to be selfish.

"She said all right," she said with a shake of her head.

"Why do I feel like that isn't all she said?"

She pocketed the phone. "Well, she said *I told you so*."

"About?"

"I told her it wasn't a date." Harley shrugged. "And she figured out it was before I did, apparently."

I laughed. "I want to hear that story."

"It's the struggle with being rebellious and having a rule follower as a daughter. She knows all the things."

"Your mom always sounds like such a fun person."

"You have no idea."

"Well, we have hours before dinner," I said. "What's the best thing to do in your town?"

She grinned. "I'll show you everything."

A local's viewpoint on their city was better than anything a tourist could manage, and we spent the next several hours immersed in her world. I loved every story and caveat and random mention about each of the locations. And as we wandered, I built a map in my mind of this Harley. The carefree city girl who could remember the name of all of her favorite ramen wait-ers, knew every street like the back of her hand, and insisted on trying more than one incredible coffee shop.

By the time we made it to dinner with Curt and his wife, Calli, we were love drunk. So many untroubled hours. No rival families. No obligations. No age differ-ence. Just the girl I'd fallen for and the big city.

We spent two hours over multiple courses with Curt and his wife. Harley carried on her side of the conversa-tion like a pro. Despite being younger than all of us, she was as smart as a whip.

Curt and I had gone to Yale, and I was pretty sure she would have kicked our asses in college. Calli enjoyed watching her school us.

Harley leaned on my arm, flushed from a glass of wine, as we headed out of the restaurant and said our good-byes to my friends.

"They're so nice!" Harley said. "That place was insane. I can't believe I've never been there."

"Yeah, Curt and Calli are the best. They keep you on your toes."

She laughed. "You're not wrong." She twirled in a circle. "What's the plan now?"

"I should...probably get you home?" It came out as more of a question than I'd intended.

Harley faced me and wrapped her arms around my neck. "I don't think so."

"No?"

"You have a perfectly good hotel room in this city. It'd be a shame not to sleep in it."

"It would be," I said as I slid my hands around her waist.

She pressed her lips to mine, and I could taste the wine on her.

"Then, we should go. And we can...sleep."

"Sleep," I agreed. "Uh-huh."

"We'll get there eventually."

I laughed and kissed her again. "You've convinced me."

We stumbled out of the elevator and onto the top floor of the Percy Tower hotel that I'd booked for the weekend. Her lips moved down my neck and across my jaw. My hands were running along her stomach and under her breasts. I tapped my card onto the pad for the door and dragged her inside.

She giggled as the door slammed shut behind us. "So eager."

"Are you not?" I asked.

She skipped across the room. Her eyes were wide as she took in the room I'd picked out. "Jesus, Chase, is this like the president's suite?"

"Something like that."

It was one of their elite penthouses. I wasn't sure how much time I'd spend with Curt and figured I'd be working up here. And probably hoping that I'd get to use it all for another purpose. The purpose that was currently running her hand along the leather furniture, inspecting the full kitchen, and peeking her head into the massive bedroom.

"This is bigger than my rental house, you know?" she called from the bedroom.

"I do not. I haven't been to your house."

She stuck her head out, the sleeve of her black dress slipping down her shoulder in invitation. "We could change that."

"We could."

She disappeared again, and I followed her into the bedroom, but she was already gone when I made it inside. Her clothes lay like breadcrumbs across the floor. One shoe, then the other, a sock, then another sock, her dress in a heap at the entrance to the bathroom.

My blood pulsed through me at the sight of it. My cock throbbing at the knowledge that she was naked only a few feet from me.

"Holy shit, this tub is insane," she called from the bathroom.

I heard a gush of water as she turned the water on. Her bra lay discarded on the tiles, and my eyes lifted to find her dangling her underwear on her finger. She tossed it toward me. Now, the only thing she was wearing was the *H* necklace I'd gotten her last year.

"Took you long enough."

"Had I known you were going to be naked," I said, my fingers working on the buttons of my shirt, "I would have joined you already."

The jetted tub was filling up fast with air bubbles bursting the surface. She stepped over the edge and sank in up to her neck. Her hair was long to her waist again and pooled around her like a mermaid.

I shucked my shirt off and went for my pants. I dropped the rest of my clothes at the tub's edge and stepped inside. My hands going to her waist and tugging her wet body against mine. She straddled my hips with a gasp. My cock jutted up between us, rubbing against her sensitive bud.

"You are a tease," I growled.

"Explain," she said, running her nose along my jaw. "I am naked and willing in your ridiculous hotel room. I cannot be any less of a tease."

"I was going to fuck you against the door," I told her. "You scampered off and got naked without me."

"Now, I'm on top of you." She bounced up and down, increasing the friction. "You can fuck me here."

"I'm going to fuck you everywhere."

"Don't threaten me with a good time."

I laughed, lifting her slippery body and angling her for better access. Then, I jerked her downward. Her pussy fit like a glove around my cock. A moan left my lips at the same time as hers. She tipped her head back, thrusting her breasts toward me. I obliged by dipping my head down and capturing a nipple between my teeth.

"Fuck," she gasped.

"You are"—I thrust upward—"absolutely"—another hard thrust—"fucking"—I held her hips down as she squirmed—"trouble."

"Only the"—she dug her fingernails into my chest—"best kind."

"You're my kind of trouble."

Her smile was euphoric at the words.

"Yours," she breathed.

"Mine."

I pulled her off of my dick, flipped her over the edge of the tub, and smacked her round ass. I gathered her hair up in my hand, yanking backward on it like a rope. She whimpered as I tugged her into place. My cock slipped against her pussy lips. She swiveled her hips against me, but I held back. Just tugged her head further back until she was tense and aching for me.

"Chase," she gasped. "Fuck...I...can't..."

"You can," I told her.

"Please. I can't..."

"You'll take this dick like a good girl, and you'll like it."

Then, I slid back home. She cried out at the force of my thrust. The pain mixing with the pleasure. Her pussy clamping down on my cock like she was going to siphon come out of my balls.

The need I felt for her was unlike anything I'd experienced in my life. The first time I'd been with her, it had felt like this was what it had always been meant to be. But two years later, it was above and beyond what that could have possibly been.

I was certain I'd built up that perfect weekend between us, but now, I knew that I hadn't done it enough justice. She was magnificent. Our day together like a beacon of light in an unlit universe.

My match.

And now, here, with her ass in the air and my cock

buried to the hilt, I wasn't sure how I'd ever survived without her.

"Come for me, baby girl."

It was only a handful of thrusts before she screamed her pleasure into the room. A flush running up her back, her sweet pussy milking me for everything it had, and then her going limp at the end of it all.

I gripped her hips with both hands and rammed into her over and over until I followed her fucking beautiful orgasm with my own.

Then, I leaned forward over her, pressing a kiss to her back.

"Magnificent."

"Mmm," she murmured incoherently.

I pulled free, and she slid bonelessly into the tub. Her eyes were glazed and delirious, looking up at me.

"Going to need this pussy again," I told her.

She smirked. "Not satisfied?"

"Satisfied? Yes." I pressed a kiss to her lips. "Sated? Never."

"I'm yours," she breathed. "Use me as you will."

"You might regret that."

"Not with you," she said, coming to her knees and running her hands up my thighs. Her tongue laved over my still-swollen cock. The mingled orgasms on the length. "Never with you."

"Fucking hell," I groaned.

Then, I hauled her dripping wet body over my shoulder and carried her into the bedroom. It was going to be a long night, and I was going to enjoy every fucking minute of it.

I woke with a mouth on my cock.

Harley's blonde hair a fan covering her beautiful, round face.

"Baby girl," I groaned. She shot me a blue-eyed look, a devious one. "Isn't your jaw sore?"

I'd given it a workout last night. I was shocked she'd want to be doing this again. That her body wasn't still a puddle next to me in a sex-induced coma.

She flexed her mouth around my cock in answer and went back to sucking me off. I dropped my head back, enjoying her mouth bringing me to full mast. I wasn't going to argue with her if this was what she wanted.

A minute later, when I was good and ready for her, she crawled back up my body. Her breasts swung as she positioned herself over my cock again. Her hand came to grasp the shaft, and I grunted in appreciation.

"What a fucking sight," I said.

She smirked as she settled herself down onto me. Her eyes fluttered closed, and her mouth opened into a perfect O. The face she'd been making as she fucked me with her mouth. A sight I would never fucking forget. Fucking gorgeous.

"You're so...big," she whispered on a sigh. "So fucking big."

I thrust upward, meeting her as she rocked up and down on me. "Made for your pretty pussy."

"Touch me," she pleaded.

My hand slipped between our bodies, a finger strumming against her clit. She shuddered under my touch as she came to life.

"Yes," she said. "Oh, yes."

"This greedy pussy is already so close." I came up to a sitting position, wrapping her legs behind me. She gasped as I used the new leverage to bounce her harder and faster, all while I got her body pressed tight to mine. "So greedy."

"I deserve another orgasm."

"You do," I agreed.

Then, our mouths crashed together. Tongues and lips and bodies, hot and wet and needy. The night before was erased by the desire still rampant between us. The feeling of never getting enough. I'd had her all night, and still, I wanted more. Always wanted more.

She came on a high, bringing me crashing down with her. Our bodies shuddering with desire. My mind going fuzzy and delirious as I held her in my arms.

"Trouble," I whispered into her hair.

"Mmm," she said, nuzzling against me. "I'm the trouble you want."

Finally, she slid off of me and went into the bathroom. She returned a few minutes later in a big, fluffy Percy Tower bathrobe, the signature *P* in gold on the right pocket.

And I realized I never wanted her out of my sight.

"Do you have to go home?" I asked.

"I thought we'd get breakfast."

"But after?"

"I should probably check in with Mom."

"Room service then. I need you at least once more before we leave."

She grinned and jumped back onto the bed, crashing into me. "I want pancakes."

"All the pancakes you'd like," I said against her lips.

"And then seconds," she teased.

"Or maybe seconds and then pancakes."

I pressed her back against the bed, and her stomach rumbled. She laughed, covering her face.

"Or maybe pancakes first," I corrected. "Can't have you hungry."

She jerked me down for another kiss, and then I went to the hotel phone to order breakfast for us. I couldn't help watching her in the bed, a satisfied smile on her lips as I placed the order.

I wondered how we'd gotten to this moment.

And how long it was going to last.

18

HARLEY

Later that morning, I was in Chase's Porsche, cruising toward my mom's house. We'd lounged in his massive hotel room for as long as I could get away with it. I wanted him all to myself all day, but I hadn't anticipated the day we'd have and needed a change of clothes. So, I was going to pop back in with Mom. I didn't have anything I had to do until Monday morning with my internship. I planned to take advantage of every single minute with him.

Plus, I was kind of looking forward to Mom's reaction to Chase.

And a little worried.

"This is the turnoff."

He shifted gears as he pulled off the interstate. "Not words I'm used to hearing from you."

I laughed. "I haven't found the thing you do that turns me off."

He smirked at me. "I accept this."

"Are you ready for this?"

"For what exactly?"

"Meeting my mom. She said she wanted to meet you when she realized it was a date."

His eyes widened as his eyes skid to mine across the car. "She did? You did not mention this before."

"Scared of parents?" I asked with a grin.

"No, parents love me."

I snorted. "Modest."

"*Should* I be concerned?"

"You took her only daughter out on a date, and I didn't come home." I raised my eyebrows. "I mean, she's going to know what we were up to."

"Fair."

"I wouldn't worry," I said with a laugh. "It's my mom."

Chase looked a little worried. Which was fine. I wanted to see him sweat for a minute. Even though there was no reason to.

My mom was so cool. A woman who had been a roadie for '80s rock bands had a fast and loose approach to parenting. After all, she'd done all the rebellion that I —her brainiac daughter—had never done.

Until Chase Sinclair…

"Well, I hope you're right."

"Guess we'll find out," I said with an unconcerned shrug.

A half hour later, Chase pulled the Porsche up in front of my childhood home. He parked on the street and jogged around to my side. I practically skipped up the sidewalk with Chase on my arm.

I turned the doorknob to the unlocked house and called out, "Mom! I'm home."

"Oh, Harley?" she asked, a note of panic in her voice. She hurried out of the kitchen with a flush on her cheeks.

"Mom. This is Chase." I gestured to him. "Chase, my mom, Tanya."

"It's nice to meet you, ma'am."

"I didn't expect you home." Her eyes jumped between me and Chase.

She was acting weird. And I didn't know what that was about. It couldn't be Chase.

"Is everything all right?"

"Oh, sure. Yes."

Then, a figure I never wanted to see again strolled out of the kitchen.

"Owen," I said in disbelief.

What in the *fuck* was my dad doing here? Not only was I no contact. So were all my brothers. He hadn't been at Jordan's wedding. Even Whitt had cut him out. And as far as I knew, so had my mom.

"Hey, honey," he said with a charismatic smile, as if nothing at all was amiss.

And maybe he could have pulled it off, but my mom couldn't.

"Mom?" I asked. "What the hell?"

"It's fine, honey. Your dad just came by to say hello."

Sure.

Hello.

I highly doubted that. Especially since I knew that my mom, for some unknown reason, still loved the man. She'd given him her whole heart, and he'd abused it to the point where she couldn't ever leave. She was too enamored with him. And I *hated* it.

"This must be your young man," my mom said in a high-pitched voice. "I was telling your dad that you were out on a date."

But Owen was looking at Chase with narrowed eyes.

"Chase Sinclair," he said as if placing Chase's face with a name.

My heart sank.

Fuck.

Fuck, fuck, fuck.

This was a disaster. A total fucking disaster. Owen couldn't know who he was. He couldn't know him from Lubbock. He couldn't know the Sinclair-Wright rivalry that had been alive over the last decade. He just *couldn't*.

This would ruin everything.

"Yes, sir," Chase said.

His eyes darted to me. An apology in them. Even though he had no reason to apologize. But he must have known how bad this was as well as I did.

"I know your father," Owen said, stepping forward and offering Chase his hand. "Arnold, right?"

Chase shook his hand automatically. "Yes, sir."

"Hmm," he said, assessing the situation.

"Well," my mom said, as if she could sense the tension in the room, "why don't I get drinks? We could... we could sit and have a chat. I'd love to get to know you."

"Chase can't stay," I said at once.

My hackles were up, and I was half ready to bare my teeth at Owen. I didn't want to be in the room for another minute with him. I didn't want to see what catastrophe he was about to wreck through my life.

But it was coming.

And I was his daughter after all.

I knew what I had to do to fix it.

"Correct," he said slowly. His eyes swept to mine again, a question in them that I couldn't answer.

"Actually, Mom, why don't you stay here with Chase? I need to talk to Owen alone."

"Uh, honey, are you sure?" Mom asked.

"Of course." I pulled Mom into a hug. Poor, helpless Mom, who just wanted the narcissist to love her. "I'll only be a minute." My eyes cut to Owen, as sharp as a knife. "Right?"

Owen smiled, an opening gambit. "Just a minute, love."

Chase put his hand on my wrist. "Harley..."

I shook him off with a smile. "I'll be right back."

I could see he wanted to disagree, but I couldn't right now. I had to be strong enough to withstand Owen Wright.

Then, I stepped into the kitchen with my father.

I hadn't seen the man on purpose in years. I despised his stupid, lying face and his ridiculous, deceitful mouth. West might have been the one to confront the rest of our family to discover the truth, but *I* was the one who had found out that Owen had a separate family in the first place. And I wasn't like Whitt, who had believed the best in him. I knew that he only had a race to the bottom.

"It's good to see you."

"What do you want?" I asked, cutting him off. My

eyes were cold, and I stood my ground against the man who had made me this hard.

"I don't know what you mean."

"What. Do. You. Want?" I bit out. "I know you have a price. What is it so that you don't tell everyone?"

"Now, Harley, why would you want to keep your relationship a secret?"

"I am not here to talk about Chase with you. Clearly, you know who he is. You know the Sinclairs relationship with our family. You know that the Wrights hate them."

"And you don't want anyone to know," he said as if he hadn't clocked it the minute he saw Chase.

"So, what do you want?"

"A relationship."

"No," I said. "You can't negotiate with ambiguity. Someone taught me that."

He smiled wider. "It's good to know some of my lessons got through to you."

"Yeah, you taught me how to be a conniving jackass. Congrats!" I mock clapped.

His smile slipped. "At least I prepared you for law school."

I sighed heavily through my nose. "All right. So, that's the play? You want to pay for law school?"

"Don't act like it's the worst thing in the world. You wouldn't have to go into debt to get your degree. That's a blessing."

Or a curse if it meant opening the door to him.

"I could get a scholarship."

"Not at Harvard."

I snorted. "I don't have to go to Harvard to be a good lawyer."

"No, but if you get in, you're going. And I'm paying."

I wavered.

I hated him for this. Hated taking his money. How he always tried to buy my affection. The stupid gifts along the way that meant more to him than how hurt I was by what he'd done. He didn't deserve this opportunity.

And if I gave him an inch, he'd take a mile.

But what was the alternative?

He would tell everyone about Chase and ruin the one thing that I wanted in this world. He'd fuck with my life the way he fucked with everything.

What were the keys to law school for that?

"Fine." I held my hand out. "You pay for law school for your silence."

"Don't make it out to be such a big deal."

"Shake on it. Or I won't believe you mean it," I snapped. "We all know you only honor your business deals and not your promises."

His face went flat. Ah, so I could hurt him. Good.

Then, he shook my hand.

"A deal is a deal. I'll be in touch."

"Looking forward to it," I said, my voice dripping with sarcasm.

I pushed past him and out of my childhood kitchen. Chase was seated next to my mom, but they both looked up when I came into the living room. Chase rose to his feet at my face.

"Give me two minutes," I said.

I all but ran into my room, tossed my clothes on the

floor, and pulled on black jeans and a tank top. I was back in the living room a split second later.

"Let's go."

"All right." He held his hand out to my mom. "It was a pleasure meeting you."

She stood and wrapped him up in a quintessential mom hug. "You too, dear."

I left the house like a tornado, set to tear the world apart, and only stopped when I reached the locked Porsche.

"Hey," Chase said, setting his hands on my shoulders. "Talk to me."

"She's not supposed to be with him. She said they weren't together anymore." I whipped around, unable to hide the fury and despair roiling through me. "He's the worst person absolutely fucking imaginable, and she's *still with him.*"

He nodded. "I understand that sentiment more acutely than probably anyone else."

"Why did your mom stay?"

"I wish I knew. She loved him. She didn't want to uproot her life."

"And now, you have a *baby brother!*" I said with a headshake.

He'd told me when his dad's mistress had a baby boy, but we rarely spoke of it. His father trotted the kid around like a trophy. The divorce had gone through, but he still hadn't married the girl. The whole thing was reprehensible.

"I'm sure the kid will hate him when he grows up. Just like you hate your dad."

"Yeah," I muttered. "This wasn't how I wanted today to go."

"No," he agreed. "What did your dad say?"

"It doesn't matter."

"I think it does since you're pretty upset."

"He's not going to tell anyone we were together."

"I wasn't worried about that."

"Oh, really?"

He sighed. "Okay. I was worried about that, but more about how you got him to agree to that."

"That doesn't matter either."

"Harley..."

"Just say what you were going to say," I said with a sigh.

"What do you mean?"

"Isn't this the point where you break it off with me?" I asked.

"That isn't..."

I breathed out through my nose. "Don't. Not right now. Just tell me."

"I talked to your mom."

I laughed hoarsely. "Oh God, what did she say?"

"That she doesn't disapprove."

"What a winning statement." Then, I threw my hands up. "As if she has any room to talk."

"She loves you, Harley. She's only worried about you. It's not like Owen."

"I know," I said with a sigh. I leaned back against the car and braced for the inevitable. "What else did she say?"

"That she doesn't want you to have to choose between your dreams...and me."

My eyes widened. "Wow. Did she really?"

"And I agree with her."

I nodded. "Me too."

"You...you do?"

"Of course. Isn't that the point of us not dating? You want me to grow up and get to decide what I want when I have a more fully developed prefrontal cortex."

"I mean, those aren't exactly the words I'd use."

"Yeah. Well, I'm not stupid. In fact, I'm very smart when it comes to everything but you, apparently." I sighed and released the tension from the conversation. I had known it was going to end up like this. I'd known, and I'd done it anyway. I wrapped my arms around his waist. "This is a dream, Chase. This entire weekend is a dream. Graduation is the end date. You set it from the beginning. I knew that this weekend wasn't going to change anything."

He held me closer. "I hate this."

I pulled back enough to slip my arms up around his neck. "I knew the weekend would end. I'd do it again."

"Me too," he breathed.

Our lips touched. A bittersweet tragedy. An inevitable conclusion met again.

I just hoped when we did meet our end date that I didn't have to make the choice my mom assumed I'd make.

My dream or Chase?

Was there much of a difference anymore?

19

HARLEY
OCTOBER

"The new album doesn't have enough keys," West said to Campbell.

Campbell, the lead singer of Cosmere, flipped him off.

"God, you're so whiny," I said, pushing my brother.

Whitt snorted, basically his agreement.

West pulled me in for a hug. "Shut up."

"A few years ago, you were dreaming of selling out venues, and now, you're complaining because you don't have enough solo moments?" Whitt asked with a scoff.

"Hey! I was playing sold-out venues," West argued.

Campbell laughed. "Yeah, at a pub in Germany."

"Those are the best fans, man."

Cosmere's latest studio album had hit all the Billboard milestones. A number one hit, a number one album, most sold vinyl in twenty-four hours that year, most streams for a new album that year, and on and on. Their tour was kicking off from Lubbock, Texas, and they'd sold out the entire football stadium with seats on the field, totaling to nearly a hundred thousand people.

I sometimes still couldn't believe it was my *brother* up there. I definitely hated that it meant he was regularly recording in LA. Touring was even worse though. He'd spend the next six to eight months touring the world.

The only time I had plans to see him between now and the end of the tour was graduation. He'd *promised* that they'd scheduled a break at the start of the summer. So, he would be home to watch me walk.

Campbell punched West after his latest joke and then headed over to Blaire. West laughed and turned back to his siblings.

"So...so..." He waggled his eyebrows. "Whitt says you're seeing someone."

I shot Whitt a questioning look. "I am not."

"You've already taken the LSAT. You applied to all the law schools in the country. You have straight As," Whitt pointed out.

"And?"

"And Bailey says you're always texting."

"So? Isn't every person my age texting all the time?"

"Who's the guy, Harley?" West asked, throwing his arm over my shoulders. "Afraid to introduce him to your brothers?"

I pushed off of him. "Y'all are assholes. Get off me with that misogynistic bullshit."

Whitt laughed. "That wasn't a denial."

"Already said I wasn't seeing anyone. And anyway, if I were, I wouldn't introduce him to you two idiots," I said with a smile and a wink.

"Wait!" West said. "It's not like we'd beat him up or anything."

"Who are we beating up?" Jordan asked, appearing with Julian at his side.

"Good luck tonight, man," Julian said with a smile, dressed as dapper as ever.

"Thanks," West said.

"Harley is dating someone," Whitt told Jordan.

Jordan turned to me in surprise. "This is the first I've heard of it."

"Because I'm not seeing anyone," I protested.

"Who is it?" Julian asked. He smacked his fist into his other hand. "We'll make sure he treats you right."

"Oh my God! Y'all are insufferable. I'm never ever telling you."

"So, there is someone!" Whitt said triumphantly.

I glared at him, but it was good-natured. Because... there wasn't anyone. There was someone I *wanted* to be seeing. But between school, law school applications, and the internship I'd taken for the year, I didn't have time to date.

I was still texting Chase...occasionally. Not enough for Bailey to be a snitch. I was going to have to knock some sense into her for that comment. Just enough for her to catch me smiling to myself around the house.

Now, my brothers—all fucking four of them—were interrogating me. As if they had the right!

"I'm done with this conversation," I said, backing up. "I hope they cut your keys solo."

"Hey!" West said, putting his hand to his heart. "Savage."

I laughed as a manager came around and ushered friends and family from backstage. I fell into step with my remaining brothers as we took a backstage exit that led to an elevator up to The Texas Tech Club, which was attached to our box. I still couldn't believe that we had a *box* for this show. I felt so fancy.

I stepped off of the elevator with Jordan and Julian in front of me and Whitt at my back. Between the sea of tall, dark-haired Wrights, I caught a swath of blond hair.

My heart stopped. Chase was here.

Fuck.

I hadn't known he was coming. He had to know I would be here. It was my brother after all. I hadn't said anything about it to him, but we hadn't spoken in a while. He'd been busy at work. I'd been getting in my final applications.

"What is Sinclair doing here?" Jordan grumbled under his breath.

Julian shrugged. "There're a hundred thousand people here. Everyone who is everyone is here. Just leave it."

"Whatever," Jordan said. "At least he's here with someone else."

My brain fizzled at the words. I'd been so focused on Chase's face that I hadn't noticed he was standing next to a very pretty blonde woman. I'd never seen her before. She was probably about his age or a little younger. She had her hand on his arm. He was laughing at whatever she was saying. So carefree.

A green monster reared up in my body.

And I was no longer in control of what I was doing.

Jordan and Julian had headed toward the box, but I was moving forward, toward Chase. My feet carrying me in that direction before I could really comprehend what I was doing and who I was doing it in front of.

"Hey," I said.

Chase turned toward me. His face went from laughter to surprise to pleased to confused. "Hey. I didn't think I'd see you here."

"No, obviously not." My eyes shifted briefly to the woman at his side. I stuck my hand out. "Hi, I'm Harley Wright."

"Hi!" she said cheerfully. "I'm Elsie Cruz."

"Yes," Chase said, as if catching up. "This is Kai's wife."

"Kai's...wife," I repeated.

Chase raised his eyebrows at me. As if to say, *What do you think?* He wasn't here with some other woman. This was his friend's wife. Not...competition. And God, I felt stupid, having thought it. He wasn't even *mine*. And yet...

"Do you know my husband?" Elsie asked excitedly.

"Oh, I just know that he's Chase's business partner."

"Well, he *was*," Elsie said, elbowing him. "Until he started working for the family company all the time. Poor Kai has been taking up the slack forever."

"We hired extra people," Chase said in apology.

"And he's not here?" I asked, looking between them.

"He's not a Cosmere fan. Bad taste, except in women," Elsie said with a laugh.

"Elsie is a huge Cosmere fan."

Elsie bit her lip. "Not to be weird, but are you the Harley that's his sister?"

"I am," I said in surprise. I'd never been recognized for my brother's fame.

"Wow. So cool. Weston is an incredible keyboardist."

"He's actually a classically trained pianist," Whitt said.

I jumped, having completely forgotten that my *other* brother was still behind me. Shit. I'd only seen Chase with another woman and gone hazy with jealousy.

Chase's brow furrowed. "Hey...Whitton."

"Sinclair," my brother said.

"Oh, I know that!" Elsie said. "I've been following Cosmere since the early days. Weston was such a good addition when Michael quit."

"He was," Whitt agreed. But his eyes were still on Chase. "How exactly do you know Harley?"

Chase glanced over at me, and I quickly cleared my throat.

"We danced at Jordan's wedding, remember?"

"Right," Whitt said. He was sizing Chase up. "You seemed friendly...like you knew each other from something more recent. I wasn't aware you knew Chase's business partner."

I could see the wheels turning in Whitt's head. Trying to fit the pieces together. Shit.

"I'm working with prelaw students," Chase said quickly. "Harley is the most promising student they have in the program."

My eyes widened at how quickly that lie had fallen off of his tongue. I *was* working with local lawyers at an internship that went with the prelaw program, but Chase wasn't personally part of it. It was tricky because Whitt could figure that out. I had no idea what he was thinking.

"How enterprising," Whitt said. His eyes came to mine. "You didn't mention you were working with a Sinclair."

"And now that I see how you're reacting, I'm glad that I didn't," I bit out.

"What's going on over here?" Eve said, appearing at our side. She nodded her head at Chase. "Hey, Chase."

"Eve."

"I need to steal my boyfriend, if you don't mind." She slung her arm into Whitt's and shot Chase an apologetic look.

"By all means," Chase said, visibly relaxing.

Eve widened her eyes in a way that said we should talk and then pulled Whitt toward the Wright box for the event.

"I should probably go, too." I nodded at Elsie. "Nice meeting you."

"You, too! Gah, can I be obnoxious and ask for an autograph from your brother?" she asked with a laugh. Chase elbowed her. "No? Okay, forget I asked."

"I'll see what I can do."

"Thank you!"

I tipped my head at Chase, who looked at me with barely suppressed want, and then walked away. Well, that had nearly been a disaster. What the fuck had I been thinking?

I pulled my phone out and sent him a text.

Quick thinking.

Was surprised you came over at all.

Yeah...

Jealous?

Me? Never!

Uh huh.

I huffed as I stepped into the box with the rest of my family. Yes, I was fucking jealous.

It was fucking hot.

I laughed and covered my mouth when people looked over at me. I sank into a stadium seat, away from prying eyes.

I wasn't jealous!

You stormed over here with your BROTHER behind you.

Not a care in the world.

Then started asking questions of Elsie.

Try again.

Fine.

Fine.

I was jealous.

Oh I know.

But if I can't have you, no one can.

He didn't reply for a few seconds, and I wondered if I'd gone too far. We'd both agreed we could date other people. Saying no one else could have him wasn't at all what we'd agreed on at any point.

I started to type out another reply, telling him I was kidding...or find a way to backtrack from my response when he said:

Fair.

My insides squirmed at the answer.

It didn't matter.

I couldn't have him right now. It was all so fucking complicated. But I wanted him to be mine and no one else's.

"Well," Eve said, interrupting my thoughts as she slid into the seat next to me, "that was close."

"What was?"

"Whitt almost realized that you and Chase were into each other."

My jaw dropped. "What?"

"Oh, don't worry. I'm not going to tell him."

"Uh...there's...nothing going on with me and Chase."

"Please. I saw y'all kiss at Jensen's election party forever ago. I thought it was way over by now, but I was clearly wrong. I had to get Whitt out of there before he realized it, too."

My mouth hung open, and not a single coherent thought came out of it. Finally, I gasped out, "No one else knows."

"It's fine." She patted my hand. "I'm a good secret keeper."

"Um...well...thanks?"

"No problem. Just be careful."

"Because he's ten years older than me?" I asked softly.

She shrugged. "I suppose that is a factor, but obviously, I dated his dad. So, I can't talk."

"Yeah, but...you were twenty-five or whatever when you were dating him."

"Great. So, I was a fully developed adult and still making horrendous decisions."

"Do you think it's a horrendous decision to be into him?"

My heart pitter-pattered in my chest. I hadn't had anyone to talk to about Chase all this time. For the first time, I wanted to divulge it all. Word vomit the years of turmoil and desire and pain and pining.

"It's a complicated one, considering your family's history with them. I'm afraid I made some of it worse."

"Arnold did that," I reminded her. "Not you."

"But now, the Wrights all hate them so much more," Eve said with a sigh.

"Don't you hate them?"

"Maybe Arnold. But Chase isn't his dad."

"No. He's not."

Eve smiled sadly. "I only mean be careful because those Sinclair men are snake charmers. They weave their way in and steal your heart. Before you know it, you're ensnared, and there's no way out."

Too late.

A few years too late.

"But I think you know that," Eve said. "You'll make the right decision."

I sure hoped she was right. Because at this point, I didn't even know what that was.

20

CHASE

JANUARY

The powder was fresh on the mountain.

It had snowed all last night, to the relief of everyone who had appeared at Holliday Ski in New Mexico. The weather was always finicky. One year, it hadn't snowed until early January despite wave after wave of promised snow.

I, for one, was glad that I'd let Blake Holliday cajole me out of Lubbock, which still had some ridiculous temperatures in the seventies for a ski weekend. The Sinclair family chalet was free, and even if it hadn't been, Blake's family owned the resort. We'd grown up together on the slopes, and he would have put me up.

"Race to the bottom?" I asked as he scooted his snow board toward my location.

"You know I'll fucking kill you, Sinclair." Blake grinned the daredevil smile that he was known for. He'd started skiing and snowboarding as soon as he could walk. I'd watched him fall face-first into every sport he could master...and then just as recklessly through women.

I hopped my board an inch forward. "Not today. I've got you."

He laughed. "Have a head start then. I'll see your ass at the lodge."

It wasn't even bravado. He was that good. He could have probably gone pro, if his family hadn't been more set on him taking over the resort. We were alike in that way.

Then, I tipped my board forward and plummeted down the double black diamond. I'd boarded this so many times that I knew precisely the route to take. Unfortunately, Blake had grown up on the slopes. He could have done it blindfolded. I was nearly to the bottom when he zipped past me, flipping me two birds.

I chuckled. I'd known it was coming anyway. When I pulled up next to him at the lodge entrance, he was already hopping off his board and whistling.

"Took you long enough."

"Yeah, yeah."

"Come on," Blake said, clapping my back. "Let's go find someone for you to fuck."

I shook my head at him. I wished that he were joking. Alas, he was not.

The only thing Blake loved more than the mountain was women. Preferably more than one at once.

We stored our boards, changed out of winter gear, and then met back up at the lodge bar. Blake had a reserved booth with whiskeys in hand and food already ordered. We were both perpetually famished after spending all day snowboarding.

I took a glass of whiskey and sank into a seat across from him.

"So, still not dating anyone?" Blake asked.

"You're not dating anyone either, Holliday," I pointed out.

He shrugged. "I'm dating a few people."

"Fuck buddies do not equal dating."

"I'm younger than you. I can still fuck around. Shouldn't you be married?"

"Why do I put up with you again?"

"Because my family owns the place," he said with the ease of someone used to getting everything he wanted.

I just laughed at him. There was nothing else to do.

We chatted over our dinner. Blake stood regularly to meet some girl or another, kiss her on the cheek, and promise to see her later. I was sure he was going to have a healthy rotation for the whole weekend before the night's end.

Me, on the other hand...

"Okay, let's loosen you up, Sinclair," he said, rubbing his hands together.

"I'm loose."

"You need to be easier then. There has to be a girl in the place you want to fuck."

"You've picked up have the bar."

"Come on," he coaxed. "Pick one and take them home. You need to get fucked. I've never seen you this uptight."

I shrugged and sipped on my refilled whiskey. "I'm not interested."

"No?" he asked with raised eyebrows. "Should I be looking for guys for you?"

I nearly spit out my drink. "That is not necessary. Just because I'm not looking to have a one-night stand doesn't mean I'm into dudes."

"I'm not judging."

"I assure you, if I liked guys, I'd let you know."

"Not my type, bro," Blake said with a wink.

I shook my head. "You're incorrigible."

"Obviously. So, say you *were* interested, which girl would you pick?"

"As if I'm at a buffet," I grumbled.

Blake shrugged. "Say you are."

"Fine."

I huffed out a breath and actually looked around the room. I hadn't even been paying attention. My eyes didn't wander anymore, like they used to. I'd never been even half as bad as Blake, but I used to at least find interest. Now, not so much.

Then, my breath caught.

Because not just anyone was in this bar.

Harley Wright was in the bar.

Her blonde hair had been chopped off short again, parted severely down the middle with curtain bangs that framed her face. A softer look than when she'd had a sharp fringe a few years ago. She was in a black leather miniskirt with a black bra top and black metal studded boots. Her lips were a bright red, and her blue eyes were highlighted by winged eyeliner, making them stand out, even at a distance.

I'd known she was going on a ski trip with her friends to celebrate the end of their last fall semester. She hadn't mentioned where but said that her friend had grown up in Denver. I'd wrongfully assumed that they'd gone up to Breckenridge. Instead, here she stood, looking perfectly and completely fuckable.

"Her," I breathed.

"Who?" Blake asked, suddenly sitting up straight. "Which one?"

"The blonde."

"Be more specific, Sinclair. Three-quarters of the room is blonde."

That wasn't true, but the hyperbole was fine.

"In the leather skirt with short hair."

Blake whistled low under his breath. "Well, damn. She's hot and *young*. I don't know if you can pull that."

I smirked at him. It was my turn to prove him wrong.

"Watch me."

Blake's eyebrows rose as I stood from the table. He definitely hadn't expected that. How could I blame him? I hadn't been interested in anyone all night. But this wasn't just anyone.

I strode across the room with all the purpose of a man possessed. Her friends whispered behind their hands as I approached. Finally, slowly, she turned toward me.

Her eyes rounded, and then a Cheshire cat smile spread on her lips. A knowing look.

Before I let myself think about it, I slipped a hand

across her waist, tugging her against me. My lips descended, capturing her in a searing kiss. The room silenced. The tittering of her friends gone. All their attention lost. And there was just Harley in my arms.

When I released her, her eyes were still closed, red lips opened slightly. Her face a mask of contentment.

Then, her eyes fluttered open. "Am I dreaming?"

I laughed and kissed her again, just as thoroughly, to prove my point.

"No," she whispered afterward. "No, this is real."

"It's real."

"You're here."

"I thought you were going to Breckenridge."

"Change of plans," she said with a laugh. "I thought you were staying in Lubbock."

I shrugged. "My friend convinced me to come to his resort because it was supposed to snow."

"*His* resort?"

"Ah, yes. Do you want to meet Blake Holliday?"

"Like *Holliday Ski* Holliday?" she asked in surprise.

I nodded.

"Um, wow. Yeah, sure."

A throat cleared next to her.

Harley actually jumped, as if she had forgotten where we were. Then, she took a deep breath and turned to the woman standing at her side.

"Uh, Bailey, this is...Chase." She gestured to me. "Chase, this is Eve's sister, Bailey, my roommate."

My mouth popped open. "Oh. Hi."

"Hi," she said with a smirk. "You're Chase Sinclair."

"I am."

She nodded and then punched Harley in the arm. "I fucking *knew* it. You little slut."

Harley laughed and shook her head. "Jesus, Bails."

"I swear it's a term of endearment and not slut shaming. Good for fucking you. Do your brothers know?"

"No," Harley and I said as one.

"But Eve knows," Harley said.

"You told my sister before me? But I'm your roommate and practically your sister." She stuck out her bottom lip. "I can keep a secret."

"Yeah, yeah. Sorry. It's just...we're..." Harley looked up at me, pleading in her eyes. As if we could explain what we were.

"On and off again?" I offered.

"Yes."

"You sure don't look *off*," Bailey said.

"Not this weekend," Harley said with a wink in my direction.

"Would you both like to meet the owner? I should probably warn Bailey off. He's a womanizer."

Bailey shrugged. "And?"

"You're only a sophomore," Harley argued.

"Again and? I'm not a prude."

Harley laughed. "Lead the way, Chase."

I directed them back to our booth. Blake was already on his feet, sizing up both girls as they got closer.

"Well, well, well, Sinclair," he said, holding his hand out, "I was in the wrong. Doesn't happen often."

I shook his hand. "Blake, this is Harley and her friend Bailey. Blake Holliday, ladies."

He was as ridiculous and gallant as ever, bowing

dramatically at the waist and kissing both of them on their hands. Bailey was looking at him like she could eat him for dinner. Harley took her hand back quickly and slid into the booth next to me.

"I hope you're enjoying my resort," Blake said, dropping an arm across Bailey's shoulders.

"It's nice," she said with a shrug. "I suck at skiing though. I gave up after the first run and decided I was going to be a lodge bunny."

His eyes widened. "A lodge bunny?"

"Is that not the term? I made it up," Bailey said with a devious grin. "I sit around in the hot tub, drink hot chocolate and apple cider, and watch everyone else wipe out. I'm a delight."

He laughed. "Well, if you want to get back out on the slopes, I could teach you."

I snorted. "Holliday, you're a terrible teacher."

"I could have gone pro. I'm a fucking fantastic teacher."

"Nah," Bailey said, interrupting.

"What do you mean, nah?" Holliday asked.

Bailey shrugged. "Not really interested in learning. Don't want to hurt myself."

"You won't hurt yourself. I guarantee that."

Harley just snorted. "I'd give up. The girl only cares about volleyball."

"I'm not going to break a leg or something and make it so that I can't play."

"Volleyball?" he asked. "Interesting. Where do you play?"

"Texas Tech. We're both Tech students."

"She walked on and is now a starter," Harley bragged. "Our little gifted student."

"Wait, students?" Blake asked, his eyes sliding to mine. "Exactly how old are you?"

"Does it matter?" Bailey challenged.

Blake's eyebrows rose. "A feisty one."

"You have no idea," Harley said.

"Something to say?"

Blake smirked. "I like them feisty."

"Oh. Well, stick around," she said, tipping her chin up.

Harley leaned her body into mine, and suddenly, Blake and Bailey's banter disappeared. It was just her against me. She slid her hand across my lap, threading our fingers together. I dropped mine to her waist and tucked her against my side. I pressed a kiss to her hair, breathing in her lavender scent.

This was what it could be like. Us out in the open, with our friends, just living our lives. No hiding from our families. It reminded me of the time we'd had in Seattle. When everything had seemed so perfect. I probably shouldn't revel in it. There were still months before graduation, but I had her to myself, and I didn't plan to let her go until she asked me to.

"Where are you staying?" she asked, tilting her head up to look at me.

"I have my family chalet on the mountain."

Her eyes rounded. "Of course you do."

"My dad got it in the divorce. Mom took the house in Cabo."

"Fancy."

"It means we can be alone," I told her.

Her eyes widened. "Now?"

"Whenever you're ready."

"Now," she repeated.

"Will Bailey be okay?" I asked, glancing at my womanizer friend in worry.

"Is Blake trustworthy?"

"He's a good guy. If a promiscuous one."

"Then, she'll be fine. She doesn't drink and can take care of herself."

"Then, let's get out of here."

"Hey, Bails," Harley said, sliding out of her seat. "We're going to head out. You good?"

"More than good," she said with a smirk that said she was not leaving Blake's side the rest of the night.

Good for her.

"Text if you need me."

"I won't. Enjoy your night."

She hugged her good-bye.

I shook Blake's hand. "Don't fuck this up."

He grinned up at me like a predator ready to go in for the kill. "I could say the same. Hope you find exactly what you were looking for."

I bumped his shoulder and then grabbed Harley's hand and headed out of there. We had much more important things to do.

21

HARLEY

"When you said chalet, I was expecting a small log cabin."

Chase chuckled behind me. "We're in *real estate*, Harley. My father does nothing in halves."

The chalet might as well have been a second lodge. The snow-topped wooden cabin had been built on the side of the mountain, looking down at the ski slopes and evergreen trees. The view even from the drive was spectacular.

I shivered in my black knee-length jacket. It wasn't the warmest thing in the world. I wasn't really used to the cold. Seattle didn't really get cold like this, and Lubbock only did on occasion. The temperatures this high up had dropped dramatically, and snow had started accumulating even more since the sun had gone down.

"Fuck, it's cold."

"Let's get you inside. That isn't exactly a winter coat. What were you skiing in?"

"Something warmer than this. But it's not as cute for the lodge bar, Chase," I teased him.

"Ah, fair."

"Plus, no tights. That was a mistake," I admitted.

His eyes went to my bare legs. "Yeah. Inside with you. We'll get a fire going."

My boots crunched along the concrete as we headed to the front door. Chase unlocked it with a keypad, and I stepped into an enormous wooden structure. The opposite wall was entirely made of glass, looking out across the ravine expanse. It was jaw-dropping.

"Wow," I whispered. The heat was on blast, and it was still cold inside from the dipping temperatures outside. "I thought our room was nice at the lodge. This is…fucking wild."

"I feel snobby saying that I'm used to it."

"You should feel snobby," I said with a laugh. "It's bananas. You're staying here all by yourself?"

"Not anymore." His arms came around my waist, and he pressed a kiss into my shoulder.

"I know that I'm a Wright, but that literally meant nothing to me until a few years ago. You saw my childhood home. I can barely fathom having this entire house as a second or *third* home. Just so you can go skiing whenever you want."

"It was my grandfather's land actually. He had a small hunting cabin on it." He guided me toward the window and pointed out off into the darkness. "You can kind of make it out over there. The cabin still stands."

"Oh, I see it! So cute. Is it still functional?"

"Well, no central heating or plumbing," he admitted. "But otherwise, yes."

"Brr," I said. "Probably not for this weather."

"No, but I used to love staying there as a kid with my grandpa. Dad had built this huge house and got pissed that I wanted to build my own fire and stay where Grandpa always stayed."

"Sounds like your dad."

"Yeah. Maybe we can go down there in the morning."

"I'd like that."

"Fire first." He walked over to the large fireplace, where wood was stacked, and began to build the thing up. He used a lighter to coax it to life and blew on the kindling he'd used to start it.

"Boy Scout," I chirped.

He grinned. "For many years," he agreed. "But my grandpa taught me how to make fires. I used to build them for him in the cabin."

"Adorable."

"Thanks...I think?"

I tugged my jacket tighter around me and hopped from foot to foot in front of the small fire, waiting for the warmth to seep into my legs. What had I even been thinking? Well, probably that I wasn't going to step foot outside.

He noted me shivering and pointed to the stairs. "The primary bedroom is upstairs to the left. You can find a change of clothes in the closet. You should get into something warmer."

"I didn't think I'd be wearing any clothes at all."

He smirked. "Plenty of time for that. I'd prefer you

not to freeze before I make you my famous hot chocolate."

"Oh? Is it from a bag that you pour into microwaved water?"

He gagged. "Absolutely fucking not. This is Dutch chocolate and cream and fucking delicious. Go. Change."

I smiled, loving this side of him, and then headed upstairs. I found the clothes he suggested and stripped out of my cute outfit for something a bit more practical— a blue Yale sweatshirt and black long johns. Not the sexiest thing I'd ever worn, but Chase clearly didn't care.

In fact, as I headed back downstairs, his eyes went molten. "That's my sweatshirt."

"Found it where you said the clothes would be."

He tugged me forward by the front of it and into the kitchen. "I like you in my clothes."

I came to my tiptoes and kissed him, deep and demanding. "I like when you take them off of me."

"That's the plan." He nipped at my bottom lip and then drew me toward the stove, where cream was bubbling in a pan. "It'll be ready soon. Warmer?"

"Much," I agreed. "I can't believe these temperatures. I was hoping for a little snow. Not a full blizzard."

His eyes went to the windows. "Yeah. It's really coming down, isn't it?"

"Guess it's good we left when we did."

"Indeed. Just fires, hot chocolate, and David Bowie."

He pressed a button on his phone, and music filtered in from a hidden sound system.

"A winning combination."

Chase finished up the hot chocolate, added marshmallows to the top, and carried both mugs over to the hearth. We cuddled up under the mountain of blankets, letting Bowie serenade us.

I took the first sip of my drink and groaned, "Holy shit."

He smirked and nodded. "I know, right?"

"Have I been living under a rock? I thought hot chocolate was mid."

"Another recipe from my grandpa. We always made it this way as kids. I can't even get it from a store anymore because it doesn't taste right."

"This is liquid chocolate. Like if I'd fallen into Willy Wonka's river."

"I'm glad you like it."

I drained my drink. Between the hot chocolate, fire, and blankets, I'd finally warmed up. I set the empty cup on the large leather ottoman, took Chase's out of his hand, and put it next to mine.

He laughed. "I wasn't finished."

"Oh well," I said with a grin.

I slid across the couch and straddled his lap. His hands landed on my ass. I ducked my head into his neck, pressing our bodies together. Just felt his heat and the solidity of him.

"I'm glad you're not in Breckenridge."

I laughed softly into his shoulder. "Same. This is way better."

"You should kiss me now."

"Forward, Sinclair."

"You like it, Wright."

I grinned and kissed him. Oh, he tasted like sweet

chocolate. And like coming home.

We should have stayed away from each other. This coming together and falling apart was so hard. I wanted it to stop. I'd never wanted it to be over as much as I did in that moment.

I was twenty-two. I was graduating at the end of the semester. My brothers might flip. Our families would certainly hate what was going on. There were so many potential consequences. But what was the alternative? We couldn't hide forever. My heart couldn't take it.

And I was so tired of hiding.

So tired of waiting.

So very, *very* tired.

I understood now what he'd meant at the beginning. I'd been a teenager. A freshman in college. Naive, young, and inexperienced. I'd had the entire world in front of me, but it'd been long enough to know that I wanted that world with him.

I'd come clean with everyone to have this all the time.

I just wasn't ready to tell him yet. I didn't want to burst the bubble that had formed around us. I'd hold off until the morning.

Right now, I'd enjoy what I had.

My hips rocked against his, creating delicious friction. My entire body was heated through now. The last vestiges of the cold gone as our bodies aligned.

"I need you," I groaned into his ear.

"Yes," was his only response.

He brought me to my feet, and we slipped out of our bottoms. Then, he tugged me back under the warmth of the covers and into his lap. I spread my legs and settled myself onto his waiting cock. My head tipped back in sweet relief. A moan leaving my lips as he dropped my hips inch after inch onto him.

"Fuck, baby girl. Fuck. You're so tight."

"Oh God," I gasped as I rocked my hips in tight circles.

His lips came to my neck, kissing his way up the sensitive skin as he controlled my movements with his practiced hands. Our bodies knew each other. Every breath, every touch, every kiss only amplified the tension roiling off of us.

"Chase," I whimpered.

"Going to come for me?" he asked, meeting my movement with an upward thrust that made my entire body shudder.

"So close."

He picked me up and dropped me onto the couch, never leaving my body. I inhaled as he hit an even deeper place. Then, he took full control, driving into me. I could do nothing but match his pace and hold on for dear life. Everything got fuzzy at the edges. The cascading waves of my orgasm building up to a tidal wave and then releasing with determined passion.

I cried out and tightened my grip on him. My orgasm triggered his own, and then he buckled as he finished inside of me. Both of us panting and desperate.

I met his blue eyes with a feeling bubbling up inside of me that I'd never known before. It was almost painful with its intensity. Like I'd looked off at an awe-inspiring landscape and known peace for the first time.

That peace was Chase Sinclair.

Was this love?

There was no other word for it. I should have been terrified because I had no idea how I could feel this when so much was still up in the air. Love wasn't fair. It didn't care that we were complicated. It simply existed wholly and completely.

He swiped my bangs out of my eyes. "You're beautiful."

I touched his cheek and drew his lips to mine. Tried to convey what I was feeling without speaking the words aloud. He met me kiss for kiss, but still, I couldn't get the words out.

"Stay," I whispered, asking for more than the night. Asking for everything.

"I'm not going anywhere," he promised.

And I wanted to believe him with everything in me.

22

HARLEY

"It's so cold," I whispered the next morning as I snuggled against Chase.

I must have kicked my feet out from under the comforter, and now, they were freezing. I pressed them against him in an attempt to get warm. He yelped and pulled back.

"Harley, you're freezing."

I shot him an apologetic look and moved in even closer. "Morning."

"Why are you so cold?" he asked on a laugh. He wrapped his arms around me and drew me into his heat. "The fireplace was on all night."

We'd let the wood-burning fireplace downstairs burn out before moving our escapades upstairs to the enormous king-size bed. The room had a gas fireplace, which regulated the temperature better than central heating. It didn't, however, account entirely for the below-freezing temperatures and snow accumulation.

"You have to warm me up."

"I'm going to do more than that," he said with a laugh.

"Breakfast first though," I murmured with a yawn. "Our late-night activities have me famished."

"I can make you pancakes. I know they're your favorite."

"Pancakes are always a yes from me."

"All right," he said, pulling away to get out of bed.

"But wait!" I said, throwing myself on him again. "I'm not ready for you to leave yet."

"Food or more snuggles?"

"Yes!" I cried.

He chuckled and wrapped me up again. "You're a conundrum."

"I want both, dammit!"

"You can have snuggles as long as you want, but I'm going to feed you. Otherwise, you get hangry."

"Don't act like you know me."

His face warmed. "Oh, but I do."

I put my hands to his stubble. "I guess you do."

He kissed me one more time and then pulled out of the bed. He slid warm clothes back on, then tossed me his Yale sweatshirt, which I pulled back over my head as he headed out. He stopped when he looked out the window.

"Holy shit!"

"What?" I asked.

"The snow is insane. I wonder if we'll even be able to get out of here to get you back to the lodge."

"That doesn't sound like a hardship."

Chase reached for his phone and clicked around.

"Yeah. Winter weather advisory. No one is supposed to leave. Guess you're stuck with me."

"There are worse things," I said as I reached for my phone and scrolled. Yep. There was a winter advisory in my messages, too. "Sounds serious."

"Good thing the house is filled with staples."

"Yeah," I said, clicking over to my email.

And then I stopped breathing.

"Oh," I whispered.

"What? Everything okay?"

"Um..."

But I couldn't say anything. I hovered over the email from Harvard Law. I'd applied to a ton of law schools, but Harvard was the deal. It was what my father had made the priority. So I'd applied, never thinking I'd get in. I hadn't even thought about it in months.

Now, I had the decision in my inbox.

They had rolling admissions that began in January. I hadn't thought that I'd hear until April. Was it good or bad that I was hearing now?

"Harley?" Chase asked, worry in his voice.

"I have my Harvard decision in my inbox."

"Already?" he asked in shock. "What does it say?"

I shook my head. Worry settled in my gut. I couldn't open it. I didn't want to know. Because no meant I wasn't good enough. Never a thing a perfectionist could stomach.

But yes...

Yes was so much worse.

Yes meant going to Cambridge in the fall. Yes meant

letting my dad pay for my degree. Yes meant leaving Chase.

"Harley? Did you get in?"

"I…I don't know," I said. "I can't open it."

"Do you want me to?"

I swallowed back the terror I felt at the momentous decision. The real fear that crept up my spine and made me feel sick to my stomach. I didn't want to know.

"Maybe I don't have to look right now."

"Hey, it's going to be fine. If you don't get in, there're other schools."

He had no idea that no was a much better alternative to yes. That yes was my real fear. Because I'd never told him about the deal with my dad. That it had opened a door I'd once firmly shut.

And through it, he'd slithered in like the snake he was. Sending me pamphlets about the program. Messaging me about essays and test scores. Offering to pay for an expensive LSAT course for the final test that I could take. Even though my July score was good enough for basically anywhere. But that wasn't the point. The money was the point. Every interaction only made me feel worse about agreeing to this.

"Harley, you're shaking," he said softly. He sank down onto the bed next to me. "Are you okay?"

I gripped the comforter with one hand. I needed to stop this. It was outrageous. I needed to buck up and find out how I'd done.

I took a deep breath and opened the email.

Dear Ms. Wright,

I am delighted to inform you that the Committee on Admissions has admitted you to Harvard Law School. Please accept my personal congratulations...

"Oh," I whispered again.

"*Oh* good? Or *oh* bad?"

"I got in."

Chase jumped up with a huge smile on his face. "Congratulations! Harley, oh my God, that's fucking incredible!"

I looked up at him. The wonder and excitement on his face. I'd gotten into the best law school in the country. Everything I'd worked for had finally come to fruition. And he was happy for me.

Of course he was happy for me.

He wanted the best for me.

But I couldn't seem to fake it. I couldn't force the joy that radiated off him. There was no happy for me in this. Somehow, it had all gotten twisted until I wasn't even sure this was what I wanted.

Chase's smile slowly pulled down. "Harley?"

I burst into tears.

"Hey, hey, hey," he said, sinking back onto the bed and pulling me into his arms. "What's this?"

"I got in," I said like the tragedy it was.

I bent forward at the waist and lay in his lap as deep, racking cries arrested my chest. I couldn't see through the tears. Or breathe through the hiccupping sobs. Or feel anything as I hyperventilated. I hadn't even known I had been holding all of this in until it erupted out of me like a volcano.

"Okay," Chase said, holding me tight. "Okay. I don't know why you're crying. But it's okay, baby girl. It's okay."

"I got in," I repeated.

"That's not cause for celebration?"

He pet my hair, brushing it gently out of my face. My mom used to do that same thing when I had a breakdown, growing up. It was therapeutic enough that my tears slowed, and I just lay in his lap, sniffling.

"I'm sorry," I whispered, swiping at my eyes.

"I don't want you to apologize, Harley. I want to understand."

I squeezed my eyes shut. Oh, this was going to suck.

"Remember when we were in Seattle and my dad saw us together?"

He tensed at the words and was slow to say, "Yes."

"Remember how I said that you didn't have to worry about him telling anyone?"

He sighed heavily. "What happened?"

I sat up, scrubbing my face clean before meeting his eyes. "Well, I made a deal with him. He wouldn't tell anyone, and...I'd let him pay for law school."

"Okay," he said.

"He said if I got into Harvard, I was going, and he'd pay."

Chase clenched his jaw. "Why would you do that? You hate him."

"At the time, it felt like the right thing to do. Like it was the only way to get him to back off. He's conniving, and I thought that I could beat him at his own game."

"But you didn't," he said, coming to his feet and

pacing away from me. "You gave him exactly what he wanted. And for what?"

"For this," I insisted.

"You did it without even telling me. Harley, you can't make those decisions for us."

"I had to." He didn't understand. He had a terrible father, but Owen Wright was his own breed of manipulative. He would have ruined everything. The one thing I wanted to keep all to myself. "I had to do it. And I'd do it again."

"So that you'd end up here?" he asked in disbelief. "Crying in my arms because your father is forcing you to go to law school." He fisted his hands. "I don't want that, and I don't want you to make decisions like that for us without talking to me."

I jumped to my feet and splayed my hands before him. Anger welled up in me. Maybe this was the wrong decision, but I'd made it in good faith, and he certainly wouldn't have been able to do better.

"What would you have done differently?"

"I would have told your brothers before I let him get under your skin," he growled.

I jerked backward in shock. My mouth dropped open. "What?"

"Do you understand? I would have walked right up to your family who hates me and told them we were together. I'd have gone to bat for us before this."

I had no words. There was nothing to say to that. Because that hadn't even remotely seemed like a possibility this summer. We were so far from that, that even hearing him say the words was a shock to my system.

"No you wouldn't have."

He blew out a harsh breath. "We'll never know now, will we?"

"It wouldn't have happened that way," I told him. "You were the one who wanted to hide that we'd been together. You were the one who gave us a graduation deadline. That was *you*, Chase."

"I know, and I still think it was the right thing to do. For you."

"For me," I said with a laugh.

"Yes, all of this was for you." He shook his head. "Look, let's step back. We're getting away from the real issue here."

"Are we? It's not the fact that we've been going back and forth for three years because neither of us can stay away from the other. And now, I'm supposed to be moving across the whole fucking country. Where does that put us, Chase?"

"It puts us exactly wherever you want us to be on graduation," he said simply.

"Does it?" I asked helplessly. "Why does it feel like I'll be a world away?"

"Harley, do you even want to go to law school?"

"I don't know," I admitted.

"You're looking at this in all the wrong way."

"Enlighten me."

He huffed. "Take me out of the equation."

"It's not that easy."

"Just for a minute. Hypothetically, take me out of the equation. Erase your father's machinations. Remove all of that extra angst about your decision." He took my hands in his. "You just got into *Harvard Law School*."

"I know," I whispered.

"The best law school in the country."

"I know."

"And you're not even a little happy?"

I bit my lip, waffling on the truth of that. What if Owen weren't going to pay for it? What if Chase weren't going to be so far away from me? What if this were just me, making the decision for myself? This was the accumulation of everything I'd ever worked for. I just hadn't been able to see through the haze of it all.

"Yes," I finally said. "Yes, I'm happy."

He blew out a breath of relief. "Good. You should be. You worked your ass off, and you're so fucking smart. Harvard should be knocking your door down to get you to go to their school."

I laughed through the tears still caught in my throat. "I got into Harvard."

"You did. You did that. No one else."

"That's impressive," I offered.

He chuckled and drew me into his arms. "It's really fucking impressive, baby girl. You're incredible."

I held on to him for dear life. My mind was still whirling. Everything was too bright, like I'd stepped out of a pitch-black room into total sunlight. I couldn't blink away the spots in my vision and suddenly felt like I was blinded.

"So, you think I should go?"

He squeezed me one more time and then pulled back. "I

don't think it matters what I want. The only thing that matters is what you want. Harvard is an incredible opportunity. You should take the time to decide that without making any rash decisions because of everything else around you."

"That's fair," I said on a sigh.

He tipped my chin up to look into his eyes. "We'll figure the rest out, okay?"

"Promise?"

He nodded, drawing me in for another kiss. "Promise."

PART III

GRADUATION

23

CHASE

MAY

I t was too hot to be in a suit.

Still, I wouldn't wear anything else. Not for a day as important as this.

Graduation day.

Our end date.

We'd been walking toward this date for three years, and now, it was finally here. All of it a mystery as to how it was going to go, too.

Harley and I had decided to hold to the end of the deal. I'd even stopped texting to give her the room she really needed to make her decision. I hadn't been lying when I said that I wanted her to make her own choices. If I'd hovered, then I would have influenced her. As much as I wanted her to be mine, I wasn't going to stop her from doing what she'd always dreamed.

But the time apart had solidified for me that I wasn't going to let her get away.

When we'd first met, she'd been nineteen with stars in her eyes. I'd fallen for her then, even when I knew we couldn't be together. And today, I was going to make sure she knew that nothing had changed.

If she'd have me.

I straightened my suit and stepped into the football stadium.

Usually, graduation was held in the United Supermarkets Arena, but after damage, they'd relocated to the football stadium. So, instead of every student only getting a handful of tickets, it was open to all their friends and family. As a member of The Texas Tech Club, it was easy for me to stroll right in.

I saw the Wrights together near the front of the stage. They were hard to miss. There were so many of them here for her today that they practically took up a whole section. Her mom, Tanya, sat between Whitt and West, who had made it back from his international tour just in time.

I had no intention of sitting with them. I certainly wasn't welcome.

So, I took a seat where I wouldn't be noticed and waited for her to walk across the stage. When her name was called, I came to my feet and applauded with the lot of them. The Wrights erupted with applause.

Harley held up her diploma, waving it at them and doing a little dance.

My beautiful girl.

I was so fucking proud of her that I could burst.

For a second, it was like she could see me in the stands. We connected. My heart stopped at her smile. And then she was continuing on her way. All of that pomp for such a small stage walk.

I headed out of the stadium before the rest of the people were announced and waited at the exit. It took another half hour before people streamed out of the stadium in droves. I worried that I might miss her, but I never should have been afraid of that.

Harley was impossible to miss.

Her lips turned up at the first sight of me. A mischievous smile that I knew all too well. She was pleased. She hadn't known whether to expect me.

"What's he doing here?" I heard Whitt snarl nearby.

I didn't even care.

I was done caring.

The Wrights might hate me. My family might even deserve it. But all I saw was her.

She skipped over to me, and I saw her brothers all peer over in confusion and outright disdain. Eve grabbed Whitt and pushed him forward. To my surprise, we were given a moment of privacy. I'd thought that I'd have to declare myself to even see her.

"Oh my God, you're here," she gasped. Then, her eyes widened, as if she'd remembered exactly where *here* was. "Oh my God, *you're here!*"

"I'm here."

"What are you doing here?" she asked with a slightly manic laugh. But her eyes never wavered from my face. She looked at me as if she'd been waiting her entire life for this moment. Euphoria replacing a fear she might have felt at having her whole family nearby.

"You know why I'm here."

"It's our date."

"It is."

"Chase!" she said with a headshake. "Do you have a death wish?"

"I had to do it."

"You did?"

I nodded. I wanted nothing more than to touch her in that moment. To kiss her. To claim her. But she was right; this wasn't the way to tell her family. This was a way for me to get run out of town. I'd only come to speak my piece.

"I want this. I want you," I told her. "I don't care about you going to Harvard. I don't care about your family. I don't care about my family."

Her eyes glistened with delight at the words. "You want me?"

"I have for three years, baby girl."

She nodded. "And my brothers?"

"Fuck 'em," I said inelegantly. She snorted a laugh. "We'll make it work."

"Oh my God," she said on a laugh. "Shut up! They're going to hear you. They're already freaking out."

"We won't tell them like this," I said. "You can tell them however you want. But I couldn't go another day without letting you know."

"That you want me," she repeated blissfully.

"I'm yours. I always have been."

She nodded. "Yes, yes, yes."

"You're mine?"

"Yes! Obviously."

I laughed, a relieved smile spreading across my face. "I want to kiss you."

"Maybe not your smartest move. I have more graduation stuff to do, but can I see you after? I have stuff to tell you. I want you to know first," she said mysteriously.

"About what?"

She glanced back then. Someone had said her name. I checked and saw that it was Bailey, wide-eyed and gesturing for her to come on. She put a finger up and turned back to me.

"I'll tell you after my party. And then we can decide how to proceed. Plan?"

"Whatever you want. We've waited long enough. What's one more day?"

She took a step backward and nodded at me. I could see her heart in her eyes. She'd wanted this for so damn long. And so had I.

Whatever she had to tell me, I'd wait for that, too.

"I'll be waiting," I told her.

She smirked. "I know."

Then, she hurried back to her friends and family. Whitt spoke to her, and I watched her shrug before she linked arms with Bailey and they buried their heads together. But Whitt turned back to look at me with narrowed eyes.

I didn't want any trouble today.

It was her day.

So, I tipped my head at the Wrights and walked away.

In a matter of hours, she would be mine.

That was all that mattered after all.

24

———

HARLEY

"He came!" Bailey gushed into my ear.

"I know. I know. Shh!"

Bailey pulled me in closer. "Are you, like, fucking freaking out? Y'all haven't spoken in months. You were going out of your fucking mind wondering if he'd be here. Or if you'd even fucking hear from him. And now, he's *here*, in front of your whole fucking family."

"I know," I said, a shiver going down my spine. "I didn't want to leave."

"I can't *believe* you didn't kiss him." Bailey shook her head. "If I were you, I'd have been half tempted to fuck his brains out right then and there."

I rolled my eyes at her. "Bailey!"

"What? You told me you did it before!"

"Yeah, but that was...not in front of anyone."

She snorted. "Well, I wouldn't have blamed you."

"Thanks. I think."

"So, what did he say? What are you going to do?"

A smile returned to my face. "He said he's all in. He wants to be with me."

"Harley, you're leaving for Harvard in a few months."

I waved my hand. "I'll deal with that. We're going to meet up after my party to talk."

"To fuck," Bailey said under her breath.

"That too," I said with a laugh. "But also to figure shit out. It's been so long. I wasn't sure it would ever actually happen."

"And now? You're going to tell your brothers? I love Whitt. He took Eve and me in when we were at our lowest, but he is going to fucking lose it. He *hates* the Sinclairs after what they did to Eve."

"I know," I said on a sigh. "He has reason to, and it's going to suck. But...I don't want to hide forever."

"Maybe just go to Harvard and be long-distance and tell them some other time, like when you're across the country."

I shot her a look. "They'd hate that even more."

"Well, it sounds safer."

She wasn't wrong. Truthfully, I didn't know what to do about them. They all had *real* reasons to hate the Sinclairs. Between Chase and Annie, Ashleigh's betrayal, the Sinclairs trying to steal Piper's winery, and everything that had gone down with Eve, not to mention Arnold knocking up an employee and only getting a slap on the wrist, I, too, hated the idea of them. It had been instilled in me early.

Then Chase had happened.

I should hate him, but he wasn't his family.

I wasn't my family either.

But half the battle was admitting that we wanted to come clean. No more hiding. And then what?

That was what we had to figure out.

And I was more than ready to do that.

Two hours into my graduation party, and I was ready to leave.

Unfortunately, I was the guest of honor.

Even though more people were congratulating Whitt and Eve on their engagement than paying attention to me. Not that I minded. I'd helped plan the proposal to get them together without Eve knowing a thing. But it was hard enough that West and Nora were getting married in a month, which was insane with his current schedule, without a second wedding to plan.

"You look ready to run," my mom said, passing me her signature cannoli.

I took a bite of the dessert. "God, these are amazing. I miss your cooking so much. Move down here?"

She laughed. "Just as you leave? You know I need to stay in Seattle for Grandma and Grandpa."

I did know. Aging parents was its own challenge.

"So," she said with a raised eyebrow, "I saw your young man at graduation."

"Oh, well, yeah."

"Is that still happening?"

"Well, no. We haven't been together, but...maybe we will be?" I offered with a hitch in my voice.

"While you're at Harvard?"

I shrugged. "See how it goes."

"I liked him," she said with a twinkle in her eye.

"Me too."

She nudged me toward the side exit from Whitt's backyard. "Go see him."

"What? Mom, it's my party."

"And? You're only half present. I know the look."

I bit my lip. "Are you sure?"

"I'll cover for you," she insisted. "If anyone asks, I can gesture wildly about feminine hygiene products and blood."

"Oh my God, Mom!"

She laughed and pushed me toward the door. "Go on. Get out of here."

I kissed her cheek and did as she'd commanded. I texted Chase on the way out.

My mom did a jail break. Your place or mine?

Yours.

I smiled. He'd never been to my place. This year, Bailey and I had rented a house only a ten-minute walk from campus. It was tiny, and parking was shit, but it was worth it for the location.

When I got home, my eyes roamed the very small first floor, checking to make sure there wasn't anything embarrassing still out. When I was satisfied, I did the same with my room. At least my bed was a very comfortable queen that I'd bought off of the previous owners. I had a feeling we were going to use it today.

Ten minutes later, a knock came on the door.

I opened it, and there he was. Still in the crisp navy-blue suit he'd worn to my graduation. But this time, he had a bouquet of black and wine-colored flowers in his grip. My mouth dropped at the display. My brothers and cousins had gotten me festive flowers that now filled my living room. Even my father had sent congratulatory pink roses—because he couldn't know me less than to send *pink* roses.

But these...

These were so me. Dark and moody with a touch of Halloween and as black as my heart.

"Wow," I breathed, taking them from him. "You did good."

"They looked like you."

"They're amazing. I've never seen flowers like this."

"I mean, they don't do black hollyhock bouquets around here."

My eyes lit up. "My favorite flower."

"So purple that it's almost black. Like a bruise."

I was half ready to toss the entire bouquet and mount him properly for that answer. He must have seen it on my face because he smirked and drew me in for a kiss.

I melted into him. Mine. He was going to be mine. All mine. Finally. Finally fucking mine. That was the mantra my mind was playing over and over and over again as his tongue roved my mouth, and our lips moved against each other, and I felt all the tension evaporate from my body.

"I missed you," I whispered.

He rested his forehead against mine. "So fucking much."

"Let's never do that again."

"You've convinced me. Even when I tried to stay away from you, it was impossible."

"I'm pretty irresistible," I teased.

He slid his hands down and grasped my ass. "That you are."

"I should show you the rest of the house." I turned in place. "Here's the whole thing."

He snorted. "I haven't seen your room yet."

My head was fuzzy with need at those words. "Well, I could show you, but we have to talk first."

"Do we?"

"Ye-yes," I stammered out as he backed me toward a wall.

"Bailey going to be home soon?"

"She...she said she'd stay elsewhere tonight," I murmured.

"Good."

My back hit the wall with a thud. His eyes were molten with desire. My mouth went dry.

"But..."

"Need to fuck my girlfriend."

He pushed his hands up the black minidress I'd worn to graduation, moving it over my hips.

"Girlfriend," I whispered.

"That's what you are, right?"

"Does that make you my boyfriend?"

The words tasted delicious on my tongue.

"Baby girl," he said, his blue eyes so vibrant, "I will be whatever you want me to be. I waited all this time for you."

"I never thought you would."

He nodded. "Remember when you thought I was with Elsie that time at the Cosmere concert? The jealousy in your eyes?"

"Yes."

"You never had any reason to be jealous."

"Well, I mean…it's been three years. I figure you were with other people."

"I wasn't."

I froze at those words. "What?"

"I haven't been with anyone else. It's you. It's always been you."

Tears came to my eyes at the words that I'd longed to hear all this time. The ones that I'd held back out of fear that it wasn't reciprocated. At the terror that it wasn't going to work out. And now, he was saying everything I'd ever wanted to hear.

25

HARLEY

The world disappeared at those words.

There was just no other way to describe it.

My soul felt as if it had separated from my body. We were spiraling upward in a floating euphoria. A heavenly anthem to our long-awaited union.

My panties fell away, his slacks dropped, and then he was inside of me. A gasp left my mouth. We'd had so much sex over the years, and nothing compared to this moment. The one where I was his and he was mine.

Him holding me up against the wall of my house on the day of graduation. Sliding wet and hard deep into me. My hands holding on to his shoulders for dear life. My climax hit me like a freight train. I clawed his back to try to get closer to him as it rocketed through me.

He just carried me back to my bedroom. We fell backward onto the queen mattress. My hands moved to his face, bringing his lips back to meet mine. Then, there was nothing but rhythmic thrusts, panting need, and the deep desire we'd felt for so many years.

Then, his fingers tangled in my hair, tugging it backward. It was the perfect amount of friction to get me there all over again. And this time, we came undone together. He bucked into me as he held me tight. Then, we both collapsed. His weight lying heavy on me.

Finally, he slid out of me and rolled over.

He panted. "Fuck, you're perfect."

I tucked myself into his side. "We're perfect together."

He pressed a kiss to my forehead. "That's right."

We were silent until our heartbeats went back to normal. Only then did I slide out of his arms and head to the bathroom. I cleaned up, and then Chase followed. A few minutes later, we were back in the bed, under the covers and wrapped up in each other. I was certain we were going to be doing the same thing on repeat all night.

His fingers threaded through my hair. So much longer than when I'd chopped it all off at Christmas. Now it was nearing mid-back.

"Do you like it long?"

"Doesn't matter to me. Long, short, bangs, no bangs, blonde, dark."

I laughed. "I've never been dark."

"Which surprises me."

"Can't be Harley Quinn if I'm a brunette."

"God, don't remind me. I never wanted to have you so bad as when you were in that outfit."

"I can wear it for you if you'd like." I trailed sweet nothings into his chest with my fingers. "You can be my Joker."

His grip tightened on my hip. "Don't tempt me."

"Oh, but that's all I want to do."

His hand came to my chin and drew me down to his lips again. We kissed like that, long and languid, as if we had all the time in the world. Because we did.

"You needed to talk to me," he reminded me after a time.

"Yeah," I said with a shrug. "I don't want to anymore."

"Because you chose Harvard?" he guessed.

"I did," I admitted slowly. "Though...that isn't all of it."

"I had a feeling you would. Cambridge is nice. I used to go to Yale-Harvard games up there." His eyes went distant. "I could probably come up once a month. I'm sure I could get away that often. My dad will hate it because the company comes first and blah, blah, blah, but we'll make it work. I still want to do long-distance."

"Chase..."

"I wouldn't expect you to come back, except Christ-mases and summers. And maybe not summers if you're clerking," he said softly, as if he was considering it.

"Chase..."

"I could be with you in the summer though. Maybe we could get a place in Cambridge, and then I'd work remote for the summer."

"Chase," I repeated more forcefully.

His eyes snapped to mine. "Does that not work for you? Do you...not want to try long-distance?"

"I don't," I told him.

His face fell, and it broke my heart to see it. "Oh."

"Because I'm not going to Harvard."

"Come again?"

"I withdrew my acceptance."

"You did what?" He came to a sitting position. His brow furrowed, and his expression was grim. "Harley, why would you do that?"

"Because I don't want to be a lawyer."

He opened and closed his mouth. "You don't?"

"I've been saying it to you for years. I don't know why it took me accepting Harvard and getting all the material and shit to really figure it out. But I spent the time that you gave me to think about it. I made my decision, and then...I realized it was the wrong one."

"But what are you going to do?"

"I'm going to work at Wright."

Chase's frown deepened. "You are?"

"I already worked it out with Morgan," I told him, mentioning my cousin and the current CEO. "I asked her not to tell anyone else yet because I wasn't ready. But I'm going to work in human resources and deal with the development of better inclusion programs. Hopefully, next fall, I'll get a Masters at Tech to supplement my work here. Maybe get a PhD later if I want to make myself even more of an expert in the field so that I can facilitate change in more Fortune 500 companies."

"And that's what you want to do?" he confirmed. "Nothing to do with...me?"

"You're a bonus," I said with a laugh.

"Well, good. I'm happy for you. I'm glad you figured out what you wanted to do. I wasn't looking forward to you leaving, but I would have been there for you."

I nodded. "I know. I just have to...figure out how to tell everyone else now. They're all so proud of me."

"You lit up, talking about what you want to do. That's all they should care about." He rubbed his thumb over my knuckles. "If you change your mind, law school is always available to you."

"I don't think I'll change my mind, but this is it. This is what I'm planning."

"You're going to be magnificent."

I snuggled in closer to him, a deep sense of relief falling on my shoulders. I'd been so worried about everything. Harvard. My dad. My future. And I decided to do exactly what Chase had told me. I took everything else out of the picture. And at the end of it, I hadn't wanted Harvard.

I mean, I had. In the sense that I'd always thought I'd become a lawyer.

But it was the name that was the draw. The sense of accomplishment that I'd chased my whole life.

It wasn't what I *wanted*. It'd have been three more years of difficult work that I wasn't even sure I wanted. Someone else deserved that spot in the end. Not me.

I was so content that I nearly fell asleep in Chase's arms when a knock came from the front door.

Chase yawned. "I thought Bailey wasn't coming home."

"I didn't think she was. Maybe she had to get something and didn't want to barge inside in case we were naked."

He laughed. "That's fair. I'll come say hi."

I grabbed my nearest black T-shirt nightgown and tossed it over my head as I called out, "I'm coming, Bails!"

Chase was behind me, searching for the remainder of

his suit so that he might be decent for my roommate. "Jesus, where the fuck did my shirt go?"

I laughed when I saw he was shirtless but in slacks. "Could you get dressed already?"

"I'm trying, Jesus. What did you do with my clothes?"

"Tore them off your body," I said with a smirk.

"Yeah, yeah."

I turned to the door and peeked through the hole. "Oh my God!"

"What?" he asked, stilling at the utter terror in my voice.

"It's my brothers."

"*What*?"

"All four of them. Oh my God, *hide*!"

Another knock on the door.

"Harley! We know you're in there!"

"Hide!" I insisted. "Go, go, go!"

Chase ground his teeth together and then nodded, hustling back into my bedroom. I took a deep breath, trying to calm my shaking hands. What in the fuck were they *doing* here?

Then, I opened the door.

26

HARLEY

"Heyyy," I drawled. My eyes tracked between my four brothers. "What are y'all doing here?"

"You left the party," Whitt accused.

"You thought we wouldn't notice?" Jordan asked.

I swallowed hard. This wasn't about Chase. They wouldn't know about Chase. I could hide this for a little longer and tell them on my own terms. Not that it explained what they were doing here.

"Mom told me to leave."

West pushed past me and into the house. "Well, I don't know why she did that, but it doesn't sound like her."

The rest of my brothers followed into the small living space.

"Come on in," I muttered under my breath as my four hulking brothers took up the entirety of my house.

My eyes skittered to my closed bedroom door and back. At least they wouldn't have any reason to go in there. Chase was safe for now. Safe until we figured out what we were going to do.

"I don't know why any of y'all are here. I just left my party. Who cares?" My voice was shaking. I didn't even sound like myself.

They were going to know. They were going to *know*. Fuck.

My brothers looked between themselves and finally nodded at Jordan.

"Owen called," he admitted.

Oh no.

Fuck, fuck, fuck.

Had he told them about Chase? Had they come here, knowing that we'd been together? Were they going to barge into the room to find him? I honestly wouldn't put it past them. There was a reason that we'd been hiding all this time. I was over this chauvinistic bullshit, but my brothers were intimidating on a good day. All four of them together, towering over me with their disapproval, was *a lot*.

I needed to take back control of this situation.

I took a step back. "I can't believe you *answered*."

"When he called all of us nearly a dozen times, back-to-back-to-back, yeah, I answered," Jordan admitted.

"I thought he was still blocked," I said.

"I still have him blocked," Whitt said. "But he got ahold of Jordan and told us what was going on."

"Told you *what* exactly?"

Please, oh please, oh please, don't have screwed up every-thing, Owen.

"Harvard," Jordan said.

I jerked back at that response. The one I hadn't at all been anticipating. Had Owen told them about our deal? If he had, wouldn't they be mad about Chase? Because right now, it didn't seem like that was the case.

"What about Harvard?" I asked.

"You withdrew from Harvard?" Whitt accused.

"Oh," I whispered.

Oh. Oh no.

Shit, shit, shit.

How had Owen already found out that I'd withdrawn? I had only done it this week, and now, he was knocking down my brothers' doors to get to me about it. Yes, I'd broken our promise. And he was within his power to break his side of the deal. Maybe it was too much to think that he was going to do the right thing. When had he ever done the right thing?

"Oh?" Whitt asked, fury building. "Just *oh*? That's all you have to say? Harley, are you out of your mind?"

"I had good reason for doing what I did."

"What could possibly be the reason?" Julian asked. "You got into Harvard Law School. You have to go."

"Actually, I don't."

"This is what you've always wanted," Whitt said desperately.

"It's your dream," West said. "You've always wanted to be a lawyer. This is like me quitting Cosmere."

"This is nothing like that," I insisted.

"It's not far off," Whitt agreed.

"Can I explain? Or is everyone going to talk over me?" I spat.

Jordan held his hands up. Julian leaned against the

sofa, uncomfortable with the direction things were going but still interested. West took a step back. Whitt looked like he wanted to punch something.

"Fine. Explain," Whitt said.

"I was going to tell everyone about Harvard tomorrow. I was accepted in January. I thought that was what I wanted to do. I spent a lot of time considering it and realized the only reason I was doing it was because it was what I'd always said I wanted. It was what all of you expected of me. I had this full-ride scholarship and a 4.0 at Tech. I should go do the thing." I gestured off in the distance. "I realized it wasn't what I wanted to do. Just what I thought I should want to do."

West sighed. "Fuck."

Whitt crossed his arms and pursed his lips. He was the guy who had the five-year plan. The one who always knew exactly what he wanted. This was anathema to his person.

"She's allowed to change her mind," Julian said.

"It's a huge change," Jordan said on a sigh. "I don't want you to regret it."

"I won't," I insisted.

"You don't know that," Whitt argued.

"I can reapply."

"There's no guarantee that you'll get in again."

I shrugged. "Then, I could go somewhere else. LSAT scores are valid for five years. So, I have five years to decide before I have to retake for new scores. That sounds like enough time to know whether or not I've made the right choice."

"Five years," Whitt said. "That's a long time. What are you going to do in the meantime?"

I grinned then. "Well, I'm going to work with you."

"Come again?" Whitt said.

"And you," I said to Jordan.

"You're going to get a job at Wright?" Julian asked in confusion.

"Correction: I already have a job with Wright."

"No," Jordan said. "I would have heard about it."

I shrugged. "Not if I went to Morgan directly. I remembered what you'd said, Whitt, when we moved here, that it felt like this was the position you were meant for. Like it had been waiting for you." I pointed at Julian. "The same thing happened for you too. Wright Construction is our namesake. Why should y'all get to claim it and not me?"

"It's not about claiming anything," Whitt insisted. "It's about you being smarter than all the rest of us combined and not meeting your potential."

I took a step back, my hand going to my heart. "Ouch."

"I didn't mean it..."

"I think you did," I said back.

"What he means," Jordan said, "is that we don't want you to waste your time."

"It's not wasting my time. I'm going to be working in HR to help with a new inclusivity program. That's what I want to be doing. Helping people and changing the world. One company at a time. I want to start with ours."

West nodded his head. Julian nudged Jordan, as if to say, *Let it be.* Only Whitt still looked unconvinced.

"How exactly is Dad involved with all of this?" Whitt asked. "I thought you were no contact."

"I was." My eyes darted to the bedroom door again. How to explain this without Chase? Fuck. "It changed last summer. He was at Mom's."

"No," West said. "She said they were over."

"Well, they're not. She...you know what? That's her story. But I saw him, and he offered to pay for law school. If I got into Harvard, I told him that I'd let him. I...didn't think that I would."

"That's a big gamble," Jordan said.

"Knowing Dad, he probably paid for a new library at the school to guarantee you made it," Julian grumbled.

"He'd do that," West agreed.

"What happened to me being brilliant?" I asked.

"Even you know he would," Whitt said.

"Yeah, he would."

I hated that I hadn't even considered it. Had I only gotten into Harvard because of Owen's resources? Did it matter now that I wasn't going? It'd be funnier if he'd donated the money and I wasn't going anyway. Sucker.

"Anyway, can one of y'all be happy for me or something?" I asked. "I've watched all of you fuck around with your lives and been there for it. Can't I do what I want for a change?"

Whitt finally uncrossed his arms. "If this is what you want..."

"It is," I insisted. "Now, all of you have ganged up on me enough. Can I tell everyone else myself tomorrow, like I planned?"

"Yeah."

"Yes."

"Sure."

A grumbled chorus of responses from my brothers. I laughed at them as I pushed them toward the door, only for a squeak to come from my bedroom door.

I froze, my eyes closing in dismay. Fuck.

West laughed. "Oh man, Harley, is *that* why you're rushing us out?"

"You have someone over?" Julian asked.

"That is...none of your business."

"Come on. Introduce him to your brothers," West egged me on.

"Definitely not happening."

"I knew you were seeing someone," Whitt said.

Then, he and Jordan strode forward at the same time, like the Neanderthals they were.

"Wait!" I called.

But the door was pulled open.

And Chase Sinclair stood in the doorway.

"Fuck," he said.

"What the fuck, Harley?" Whitt snarled.

"Fuck," I said softly.

"This isn't what it looks like," Chase said with his hands up placatingly.

"What does it look like?" Jordan demanded. "Because it looks like you're screwing our sister."

"Jor!" I snapped.

"Harley and I are together," Chase said.

Claiming me.

In front of all of my brothers.

I swooned.

"Like hell you are," Whitt said.

"Fucking hell, man. How low will you stoop to get back at me?" Jordan demanded.

Chase's eyes narrowed in anger at the comment. I couldn't even believe Jordan would go there. This had nothing to do with Jordan and Annie. Or Chase's relationship with Annie. That had all been over so long ago.

"Who the fuck do you take me for?" Chase snarled.

"A Sinclair—a fucking lying snake!" Jordan said.

He took one more step forward and swung his fist into Chase's face. A crack sounded in the tussle. Blood poured out of Chase's nose. My brothers rushed forward to pull Jordan off of him. West pushed past Julian and tried to get his licks in, but Chase had taken a step back.

In all of it, I stood there wordlessly.

Forgotten in the wrath. Discarded in the mayhem. Left to stand sentinel for my brothers' fury against the man I loved.

I stood, wondering how it had all gone so irrevocably wrong.

And I saw no way to fix it.

None at all.

Not without burning it all down and starting anew.

So, that was what I had to do.

To Be Continued

Thank you so much for reading WRIGHT KIND OF TROUBLE! I loved writing the beginning of Chase & Harley's story! But I couldn't stop at just one. I wanted to keep writing them forever. So you get a whole other book about them in: **Wright Kind of Love**

"The conclusion to the Wright duet age gap romance from USA Today bestselling author K.A. Linde.

Chase Sinclair should be my enemy. Wrights and Sinclairs don't mix. Not with years of history and turmoil between our families. A rivalry that only seems to fester and corrode with time.

Except I'm done denying what I want. We both are. Just when we think we have it figured out, it all blows up in our faces.

But we're determined to make this work. Even knowing that the road ahead is uncertain. And everyone wants us to fail. At least we're doing this together. Everything is on the line. Our friends, our families, our careers. And we'd give it all up.

He may be from the wrong family, but he's my Wright person.

ACKNOWLEDGMENTS

Thank you to those who encouraged me to make this a duet. I had so much that I wanted to do that I knew if I made it one book it was going to be a monster of a book. I was afraid that I wouldn't be able to do it justice. But I love Chase & Harley so much that I'm glad I gave them double the spotlight. They deserve it!

The soundtrack to this book was: 1989 vault tracks from Taylor Swift especially Say Don't Go, bad idea right? by Olivia Rodrigo, Holding Back My Tongue by SEOAN, and Maisie Peters.

ABOUT THE AUTHOR

K.A. Linde is the *USA Today* bestselling author of more than thirty novels. She has a Masters degree in political science from the University of Georgia and served as the head coach of the Duke University dance team. She loves reading fantasy novels, binge-watching Buffy, traveling to far off destinations, baking insane desserts, and dancing in her spare time.

She currently lives in Lubbock, Texas, with her husband, son, and super adorable puppy.

Visit her online:

www.kalinde.com

Or Facebook, Instagram & Tiktok:
@authorkalinde

For exclusive content, free books,
and giveaways every month.
www.kalinde.com/subscribe

www.ingramcontent.com/pod-product-compliance
Lightning Source LLC
Chambersburg PA
CBHW061242310726
48971CB00007B/2180